Sword

By

Steven A. McKay

Copyright ©2020 Steven A. McKay

All rights reserved. No part of this book may be reproduced,
in whole or in part, without prior written permission
from the copyright holder.

ALSO BY STEVEN A. McKAY

The Forest Lord Series:
Wolf's Head
The Wolf and the Raven
Rise of the Wolf
Blood of the Wolf

Knight of the Cross*
Friar Tuck and the Christmas Devil*
The Prisoner*
The Escape*
The Abbey of Death*
Faces of Darkness*

The Warrior Druid of Britain Chronicles
The Druid
Song of the Centurion
The Northern Throne
Over The Wall*

LUCIA – A Roman Slave's Tale

Titles marked * are spin-off novellas, novelettes, or short stories.

All others are full length novels.

Acknowledgements

Thanks to Bernadette McDade and my editor, Richenda Todd.
And a big 'thank you' to my wife, Yvonne, for helping me with the title of the book.

Prologue

Henry of Castellford was not a poor man. He'd fought bravely in King Edward's army against the Scots twenty-five years ago and been rewarded for his service with a little parcel of land near Pontefract that brought him a steady income every year. Although, at the time he had little experience in farming, he hired a good bailiff who managed his holdings well and his wealth had grown over time, along with his own family.

He looked out across the sea, breathing the air deeply and smiling at the fresh scent which reminded him so strongly of his childhood. He would have liked to see the soaring gannets for their cries, like the smell, reminded him of happy times, but they weren't here during the winter. He wondered idly where they disappeared to every year, but the sight of a robin fluttering about the frost-rimed grass to his right distracted him, and he watched the little bird until it disappeared into the undergrowth.

The sea calmed him and helped him gather his thoughts; it always had, since he'd been a boy living in the tiny village of Newsham coming here to sit on the cliffs and throw stones into the foaming spray below when the tide was in, or watching the birds search along the beach for shells to crack open when the waters receded.

He felt calm now, as he thought fondly of his two children, adults now of course, and their mother, Elaine, who had been taken from them four years ago by a cruel wasting disease. He missed her still, but they'd had good years together, which was more than many people could say, especially given the famines and violent raids by the Scots back in those first, early years of their marriage.

A small fishing boat was visible on the horizon and Henry watched the men at work. They were too far away to make out properly, but the sun was setting and he knew they would be sailing for home soon. He shivered and pulled his cloak tighter around his shoulders, wondering if it would snow that night. Probably – the winters had been colder recently he thought, although perhaps that was just his age catching up on him.

Forty-three years on God's Earth. He didn't feel old, other than a bit of stiffness when he got up in the mornings; yet, when he caught sight of himself in the solitary mirror in his home he noticed lines around his eyes that hadn't been there when he was younger and his hair was thinning, but whose wasn't?

That thought reminded him of the woman he'd met not long after his wife died: Alice de Staynton. It had been her thick brown hair that had first drawn his attention, and her easy smile and warm nature had caused him to fall in love with her, despite the fact his children did not like her. They didn't understand how lonely he'd felt though, and how Alice had filled a void in his heart.

As it turned out, Alice was part of a religious group, the Disciples of God, who gathered in a converted barn not that far from Henry's own village to pray and sing the glory of Christ. He'd gone along with Alice to watch their meetings and found himself enthralled when they spoke of fighting evil spirits.

He'd heard such sermons before from priests, but those had bored him, whereas the Disciples of God's meetings filled Henry with a righteous excitement and anger against the evil forces that beset the world.

He felt as though he'd discovered a new life, and spent more and more time with Alice and her group, much to the chagrin of his children. His jaw clenched as he thought of Nigel and particularly Elspeth's increasing hostility towards Alice. Selfish, that's what they were, but he didn't need their approval to wed her and that's what he'd done, discovering a happiness and love that he thought only happened once in any person's lifetime.

It didn't even matter that the Disciples of God lived a chaste life, so he and Alice could never consummate their marriage. He was just happy to be with her.

But then the headaches had started.

At first, he thought it was a result of too much ale. He'd always been fond of a good drink and, after almost three decades of drunken nights, he was sure it was catching up on him, so he'd stopped imbibing as much. It had helped a great deal with his general health, but didn't stop the headaches, so Alice insisted he speak with an acquaintance of hers – a barber-surgeon from York. The man examined Henry thoroughly and told him he had something growing inside his head. The only way to relieve the pressure would be to drill into Henry's skull, which would probably kill him faster than the illness.

Henry could remember well the sensation of cold terror that had swept through him at the surgeon's words. He would not let the man drill into his head, but he did not want to die in the way described to him, a long and lingering death that would rob him of his faculties and his dignity. The Disciples of God prayed for him of course, but it had been of little use for the headaches did not abate and, eventually, he came to terms with his lot.

He sighed heavily and looked up, watching clouds scudding across the face of the newly risen moon and experiencing the same sense of awe he'd felt since he was a child at the sight of the twinkling stars. The universe was truly a wonderful place, and a terrible place.

"Our father, who art in Heaven." He stood up, and remained perfectly still while he recited the Lord's Prayer, feeling God's love in every part of his body as he stared out across the moonlit sea.

And then he stepped forward off the edge of the cliff and hoped his sacrifice would be rewarded as promised.

PART ONE - WINTER 1329

CHAPTER ONE

ALTOFTS, YORKSHIRE – AD 1329

The gap-toothed man threw a punch that connected with the bicep of his target, but his sense of triumph was short-lived, as he immediately found himself flat on his back with a shattered nose and a horrible ringing in his ears.

Thankfully, however, the bailiff couldn't waste any more time on him, for another thug had just pulled out a knife and that really enraged the giant, bearded lawman who was, rather ironically, known as Little John.

"You big bastard, coming here demanding money when you were a damn outlaw yourself not so long ago!" The knifeman lunged forward, thrusting the tip of his blade at John's midriff, but the bailiff was well trained and well used to this sort of violence and he easily batted the knife aside before reversing his quarterstaff and clattering it against the side of his opponent's head.

The sound of heavy breathing was all that could be heard now, as John looked down at the pair he'd so easily incapacitated and then around at the watching villagers, most of whom were grinning at the unexpected entertainment. The people knew the bailiff well and not only respected him, they liked him, even if it did sometimes irritate them when he came to Altofts on the sheriff's business. Today wasn't a problem though, for the two men he'd downed were well-known local layabouts.

"About time someone put Clibert on his arse," someone muttered to grunts of agreement. "Serves him right for drawing a knife. That ain't right."

"'E's lucky the bailiff didn't crack his skull open."

"Aye."

"Bloody wish he had."

John shook his head in amusement. His job was not always this easy – in villages and towns where he wasn't quite as well known the locals could get upset in a situation like this, so he was glad to have sorted things out without being injured himself, or causing a riot. He poked the tip of his quarterstaff which, at over six and a half feet in length was as big as he was, into the belly of the man whose nose he'd broken.

"Get up and be on your way, Fulke, you ugly bastard, before I remove your last two teeth."

Clutching his bleeding nose, the gap-toothed little man got to his feet, warily eyeing John the whole time, and then, somewhat unsteadily, walked away towards the centre of the village where, no doubt, he'd find a pot of ale to calm his nerves and silence the ringing in his head.

The bailiff turned his attention to the second, taller man, Clibert, who was still lying, silent and unmoving, on the road.

"Hit him again," someone called gleefully, drawing laughs from others in the crowd.

"Aye, kick him in the nuts!"

John grinned but didn't heed their advice. Instead, he bent down and began searching the unconscious fellow's clothes for the money owed to the Crown. Clibert had been found guilty of stealing a dog from one of his neighbours and ordered to pay a fine which, of course, he'd never done, hence John's visit that day. It wasn't even that much of a fine, just a couple of shillings; hardly worth the headache he'd have when he finally woke up, but that's what happened when you tried to stab someone like Little John.

He grunted as his fingers closed around a heavy bag in a pocket sewn into Clibert's tunic. He didn't even need to open it to know what was in it, it was obvious from the shape of the contents: coins.

He looked up at the villager who'd been most vocal in his desire to see the dog-thief beaten, and showed him the bag of money. "Does he always carry this much money about with him?"

The surprised frown on the villager's face told its own story, and the bemusement was reflected in the expressions of the other members of the crowd.

"He's never got a penny to his name," the man John had addressed said suspiciously. "Or at least, so he says when he's in the alehouse trying to mooch free drinks from folk. I've no idea where he's found that, but I'll wager he's not earned it from an honest day's work."

John got to his feet and fished around in the leather bag, eyeing the small silver coins and estimating their total value at about four or even five pounds—more than a carpenter like Clibert could earn in a month or two, even if he actually worked every day. Then he took out a couple of the pennies and handed them to the man in the crowd.

"Here. You and your mate there, carry him to the alehouse for me. I might as well have a drink while I wait on him waking up."

"You buying a round, bailiff?" a woman cried. "There's plenty in Clibert's purse there to pay for a drink for us all. God's blood, he owes us all enough."

"No," John replied, but his good humour had been dampened somewhat by the silver he'd discovered. Something didn't seem right to him and he didn't like it when that happened. "The money will go towards the fine he owes. The rest, well…" He moved off, following the pair who'd lifted the unconscious Clibert and were now bearing him, none too gently, towards the alehouse. "I'll need to find out where he got it all before I can decide what's to happen with it."

The crowd dispersed, encouraged by Little John, and by the time they reached the alehouse only a couple of dirty-faced urchins followed, in hopes of a coin being tossed to them. They were out of luck, and so was the man whose nose the bailiff had broken, Fulke. He was sitting nursing a drink when John shoved the door of the alehouse open, and decided it was safer to leave when his friend was carried in and dumped unceremoniously on the floor.

"Thanks for the help, lads," John said, gently but firmly shoving the two helpful villagers towards the doorway behind Fulke. "Off you go now. I'm sure I can handle this one by myself. You best be about your work." With that, he closed the door on them and turned back to the man on the floor who was, finally, starting to come around.

"Two ales," John said, placing a coin from Clibert's purse onto the counter. "And then be about your business, if you would. I want a word with this one. Alone."

The thin-lipped innkeeper seemed like he might argue, but the look in John's eyes quickly changed his mind and he lifted the coin then went to fetch the drinks without a word. After carrying the ales across to the table, he flicked his stained rag over his shoulder and disappeared out of the back of the little building, muttering to himself about needing to prepare something for dinner.

John took a long drink of his ale – so long, in fact, that he emptied it. It was dark and tasty, despite the sweet smell of the herbs that had been added to make it appear fresher than it really was. Clibert pulled himself up onto a stool near the bailiff, rubbing his balding head and looking about the empty alehouse fearfully, as if expecting another brutal attack. He reached out to take the second mug of ale, but John snatched it away and sipped it, eyes twinkling.

"If you want a drink," the bailiff growled. "You better tell me where you got all this from." He dropped the purse of coins onto the table with a thump. To his surprise, Clibert didn't look shifty, or even nervous. On the contrary, he looked at John with a smug expression. He had a pale, round scar from an old burn beneath his eye, and it stayed oddly flat and smooth as the rest of his face creased in a smile.

"I earned that honestly," he said, with such conviction that John, who was a good judge of a man's character, actually believed him.

"What you think is honest probably doesn't match my definition of the word," the bailiff growled. "What exactly did you do for this?"

"Helped clear the ruined old church a couple of miles north of the village," Clibert said, wincing as his injured temple suddenly flared with pain. "Some new religious group's taken over and the woman that runs it asked me to help fix it up."

John frowned, trying to place the church Clibert was talking about. He knew this whole area better than most, having spent years travelling around as an outlaw, learning the secret paths and hidden places, so it didn't take long before he had a picture of the building in question in his head. St Joseph's. It wasn't exactly a ruin, since its walls remained mostly intact, but parts of the roof had fallen in and the interior was a mess. It had fallen out of favour when a newer church was built in a location easier for the parishioners to reach and eventually been abandoned.

"What religious group?"

Clibert shrugged. "The People of God or something. I dunno, I didn't take much notice of them."

"And they paid you all that to clear an old building?"

The man frowned at John's incredulous tone. "You might not have a high opinion of me," he said. "But I'm a carpenter by trade. I got rid of all the debris from the roof and so on, then helped repair it, with Fulke labouring."

John watched Clibert as he spoke, sensing he was telling the truth but also that something was being held back. "I'll pay the place a visit," he promised. "And if I find out you're lying I'll be back here to take you to the sheriff." He stood up, towering over the villager, whose previous confidence quickly evaporated at the sight of the bearded giant gazing malevolently down at him. "You should pay the place another visit too, and offer God a prayer of thanks that I didn't beat the shit out of you for trying to stab me."

He emptied the ale mug and slammed it onto the table, then headed for the door without another word.

"What about my drink?" the bruised carpenter asked indignantly. "You nearly killed me with that damn quarterstaff of yours, bailiff. The least you can do is buy me an ale to steady my nerves."

John was about to reply when the door was thrown open, nearly crashing into him, and, instantly, his great quarterstaff was brought round defensively before him, ready for this new challenge.

The villager who stared into the gloomy interior of the alehouse was no threat though, far from it. He looked at the bailiff and gestured excitedly. "Quick, John. You'll want to see this – it's the new people from St Joseph's. And they're carrying a dead nobleman!"

CHAPTER TWO

Little John walked out of the low building and watched as a procession of sorrowful-looking people passed. There were nine women and six men, with seven of the party carrying the body of a man on a crude stretcher while a lady walked ahead of them singing soft prayers. It was a strange sight and the people of Altofts, including John, looked on in bemusement as the strange group walked on towards the north without stopping.

John sensed a presence at his back and glanced round to see Clibert standing there.

"Is that the people who hired you to sort out St Joseph's?"

"That's them," the carpenter agreed, drawing himself up proudly, as if his work at the ruined church had been his only recent employment. "The woman at the front's their leader."

"And the man on the stretcher?" Usually, a dead person's face would be covered but, for some reason, not this time. Some odd custom this group observed, perhaps.

Clibert shrugged but there was a shifty look on his face. "Couldn't tell you who he is –" he cackled suddenly. "Who he *was*, I should say, eh, bailiff? Ha!" With that, the man rubbed the egg-sized lump on his temple gingerly and disappeared back into the alehouse, slamming the door at his back.

John didn't need anyone to tell him who the dead man was though, for, although the corpse was bruised and in poor condition, he now recognised Henry of

Castellford. The bailiff was torn, desiring to talk with the very people who'd literally just walked past him but not wishing to disturb their solemn procession.

He presumed they were taking Henry back to his home, in the village that was once a Roman fort near Pontefract, but then, that was to the east, and he could see them still heading to the north. They had to be going to the church Clibert helped refurbish.

Well, the bailiff's business in Altofts was done and it was early enough that he didn't have to head for home yet, so he decided to collect his horse and pay a visit to St Joseph's. The place was apparently empty, since the religious group were here, so he could get there ahead of them and have a look around. He had no real jurisdiction since the Sheriff, Sir Henry de Faucumberg, employed him as a roving lawman, with no ties to one particular area. He basically went from place to place collecting fines from troublesome or violent offenders but...something bothered him about these people who'd taken control of a dilapidated church and paid a known layabout a lot of silver to tidy it up for them.

His old friend Will Scaflock would undoubtedly accuse him of being a nosey bastard, and John smiled for Will would have been right. But he'd also learned to trust his instincts, and he felt he should at least go to St Joseph's and find out what had happened to Henry of Castellford since, judging by the state of his face, his death had not been a peaceful one.

He found his horse where he'd tethered her near the blacksmith's, and the smith grinned and waved when he saw him, asking if his business there had been successful. John was well known to the blacksmiths of Yorkshire, since he'd been one himself in his younger days.

"Aye, Eustace ," he called, smiling in return. "All sorted. Did you see the religious folk passing? D'you know anything about them?"

The smith walked to the front of his shop, sweating profusely, muscles in his arms cording as he hefted his iron hammer up onto his shoulder. He shook his head thoughtfully. "Not really. They bought some nails and tools from me when they were sorting out St Joseph's. Tried to get me to come along and join their meetings but I do enough praying as it is."

John laughed. "Aye, I know what you mean. Once a week in the church is more than enough for me."

"Why do you ask? They not paid a fine or something?"

John shook his head. "Oh no, nothing like that. I just saw them passing with the bier and wondered what their story was."

The smith waved as the bailiff untied his horse and dragged himself up into the saddle. "Farewell, John," he called. "I think it can only be a good thing that those people have taken over the church. It's a fine old building and deserves to be looked after. Rather a religious conclave using it as a home, than a bunch of damn outlaws. No offence."

John laughed again as he kicked his mount into a canter. "None taken. But don't forget – we were *good* outlaws!"

The acrid smell of the smithy was soon left behind along with the rest of Altofts as John rode north. He took a roundabout route towards St Joseph's skirting the main road and the well-worn pathways, avoiding the funeral procession that was now out of sight. At the speed they'd been moving he should reach the church a few minutes ahead of them since it was only a mile or so away, and that would give him enough time to take a look about the place without anyone there to hinder him.

His unruly brown hair and beard were swept back by the wind as he gave his mare her head, galloping through a field that had been left fallow after the autumn harvest, providing him with a surface safe enough to travel quickly upon. St Joseph's soon came in sight and he was glad to see no-one in the grounds which, he had to admit, looked neat and tidy compared to the last time he'd ridden past the place a few months earlier.

There were a few gravestones on the grass behind the freshly painted gates, some of which had fallen down over the years but now were upright again, and there were even some late blooming flowers, which gave the place something of a cheery look. Or perhaps they'd always been here, hidden behind other, less pleasing foliage and the new occupiers had pruned the branches and leaves until the colours were brought out. Certainly, these 'People of God' as Clibert had called them, seemed to have restored the place to something of its former glory.

He slid down to the ground and tethered the mare to a small bush so she wouldn't wander off, then he unclipped his quarterstaff from the saddle and turned to properly take in St Joseph's.

A single storey building built from grey sandstone with a small tower, it would never rival York Cathedral as the most impressive place of worship in the area, but there was something homely about it. Welcoming. This was the kind of place John thought God would choose to reside, rather than some grand structure that cost a fortune to build while the poorest people in England starved.

He shook his head, remembering why he was there and wanting to make the most of the few minutes he would have before the People of God turned up with the body of Henry of Castellford, and practically ran to the great wooden doors on the western side of the building. Expecting them to be locked, he was surprised when they pushed open easily. He'd thought he'd have to pick the lock, a skill he was fairly proficient in nowadays, ironically, having learnt how to do it long after his time as a thief in Robin Hood's gang were behind him. Silently, though, as if the hinges had been freshly greased, the doors opened at his touch and he hastened inside.

Afternoon sunshine streamed in through the simple stained-glass windows in the north and south walls – no fancy scenes from the Passion of Christ here, merely plain coloured panels – and John gazed about, noting the lack of pews in the nave. Even the altar, which should have been in the chancel at the far, eastern end of the building, had been removed at some point. In its place was a small firepit, with a cooking pot suspended above it. Looking up, the bailiff noticed that the roof had been modified there, with the addition of a roughly cut hole to let the smoke out. Only a little sunlight came through and John suspected a crude covering had been erected outside to stop rain coming in. It looked a hasty job, undoubtedly completed by Clibert.

The removal of the altar surprised John, although he wondered why. A fire would be needed for warmth and cooking after all, and the new owners weren't going to run the place as a church, were they? Not from what little he'd been told – he assumed it would just be a place for the group members to live and spend time doing... whatever it was unofficial religious groups normally did.

He walked slowly from one end of the place to the other, just looking around, noting the pungent scent of incense in the air and checking the floor for...He wasn't really sure what for, but he had a distinct feeling there was something odd about the place. Perhaps it was nothing more than his imagination; he did tend to see mysteries where there were none nowadays, after the recent trouble at Croftun Manor, where a nobleman had been tormenting his wife. John, with the help of his old friend, Friar Tuck, had managed to solve the mystery and set things right and it had been such a satisfying experience that John had unconsciously started looking for other conundrums that might need solving.

There seemed to be very little here, however. Some blankets were piled up in the north transept, suggesting the members of the group actually slept here, and there were some barrels and crates which looked as though they held food and drink in the opposite transept. Nothing looked suspicious or out of place and John began to feel slightly foolish, and guilty to have come here when he hadn't been invited.

He noticed a door which had recently been fitted with a new lock—another of Clibert's jobs no doubt—and, seeing no key hanging nearby, shoved it hopefully. It opened to his touch and he went through into what was probably the vestry originally.

It was darker in this room, for there was only one window and that was rather small. It offered enough illumination, however, to let the bailiff see the cudgel slashing through the air towards his forehead.

Instinctively, he brought up his quarterstaff, knocking the blow aside but, before he could lash out himself, a fist crashed into the side of his face and he roared with fury.

"Break into a house of God, would you?" a voice heavy with righteous anger demanded. "Well, you'll regret coming here, you great scruffy oaf."

The cudgel came for him again, and again he knocked it away, but something hit him square on the back of the head and white spots exploded before his eyes. Struggling to retain consciousness, he jerked his elbow back, feeling it connect with a satisfying thump in the midriff of the attacker behind him. Pain engulfed him though, and he closed his eyes, only to be thrown sideways by a brutal kick, and he knew the fight was lost.

"I'm the bailiff!" he shouted, raising his hand up over his head as another kick hammered into his ribs. "A lawman!"

But his words had little effect and the blows continued to rain down on him until even the bright stars in his vision turned black and he could feel nothing anymore.

CHAPTER THREE

His hands were tied behind his back; he could feel the ropes digging into his skin painfully, but the throbbing in his skull was more worrying. He lay still, eyes closed, listening and trying to come fully alert without rousing his captors.

Why had he expected to just walk in here and wander about as if he owned the place? He knew better than anyone that Yorkshire and Nottingham had their share of roaming outlaws. When he found the door to St Joseph's unlocked he should have realised someone was probably inside.

Then another thought struck him. He'd cried out that he was a bailiff, assuming his attackers were lawful citizens who wouldn't want to injure one of the Crown's servants. But what if the men who'd knocked him unconscious were robbers, who'd broken into the church before he turned up? If that was the case, his chances of survival were slim.

He risked opening one eye just a crack and realised he'd been brought back out into the main part of the building. No one was around and he couldn't hear any sounds of movement either, so he began flexing his muscles, trying to loosen the ropes around his wrists.

"Oh, he's awake."

John froze, although his efforts had been fruitless anyway for, despite his prodigious strength, the ropes binding him were too strong to break or even wriggle out of in such a short space of time.

The two men came in via the same main, double doors that he himself had entered through and he saw them in the light, clearly, for the first time. His immediate thought was that they were not robbers after all, for they wore drab grey robes like many clergymen. His second impression was that they looked more like soldiers than monks, which almost made him smile when he thought of his own friends, Friar Tuck, and Will Scaflock, both of whom had been soldiers and men of God.

They walked over and stared coldly down at him.

"Well, I've told you I'm a bailiff," John said. "My name's John Little. Are you going to untie me?"

The men looked at one another and their grim expressions did not change. They were both in their mid-twenties, John guessed, and shared the dour faces many zealots had. Life was a serious business to them, and every action was taken with a view to serving God. What this particular religious group taught in terms or mercy or justice was a mystery to the bailiff however, and he surreptitiously began working his fists again in an attempt to free himself.

"Does being a bailiff give you the legal right to trespass?" one of the men demanded. He had very closely cropped hair and piercing blue eyes and John marked him as the more dangerous of the two. "What were you doing in here anyway?"

"Just looking around."

"Snooping," the man retorted, bending down and lifting John's quarterstaff from where they'd left it on the floor. He eyed its length, hefted it, and then clattered it against John's thigh, drawing a yelp of pain from the bailiff.

"Well?" the other acolyte said, leaning down on his haunches and staring into John's eyes. "Are you going to tell us what you were looking for? Or do we have to break a few bones with your own staff?"

"I thought you were the People of God?" John asked, frowning more in surprise than fear. "Is this how you usually treat visitors to your...community?"

Silently, the man with John's quarterstaff lashed out again, this time striking John in the shoulder and drawing an even louder roar from the flushing bailiff.

"When I get out of this, I'm going to ram that staff so far up your—"

Behind him, the main doors opened again, letting yellow sunshine stream inside, contrasting with the blue, red and green luminescence cast on the floor by the stained-glass windows. The acolytes seemed to forget about their captive, dipping their heads and staring at the floor as if Christ himself had wandered into the old church.

There were soft footsteps and John, feeling like a lump of wood in his trussed-up state, craned his neck to see who was coming for him now. It was a woman, and she stopped beside him, eyeing him coolly.

"Disciples of God."

John's forehead creased. "Eh?"

"We are the Disciples of God," she said, in a soft, melodious voice. "Not the People of God, as you called us a moment ago." Turning to the two men, who still stood with their eyes downcast, she asked them what was happening.

"We were in the vestry, sorting out the scrolls, Holy Mother," replied the one holding the quarterstaff. "When we heard someone coming into the church. This fellow wandered about, as if looking for things to steal, and then he had the audacity to come through, into the private area."

"Look," John growled impatiently. "I'm not a bloody thief—"

"Mind your language please," the woman chided, turning back to meet John's glare. "This is a sacred place after all."

Her voice was strangely soothing, and John felt almost like a naughty child as she eyed him with a small smile tugging at the edges of her mouth. It was the woman who'd led the funeral procession through Altofts. She was middle-aged and slightly plump, but had a confident manner that John found reassuring. The scent of rose-water drifted from her too, which was most pleasant considering he, and the two male Disciples, smelled of mostly battle-sweat and leather.

"I'm a bailiff, er, Holy Mother," he said, still feeling foolish and powerless and wondering what exactly these people were going to do with him. "I was in Altofts earlier on the Sheriff's business, and heard your group had taken charge of St Josephs. I just came for a look; it's my job to know what's happening in the lands hereabouts. When I found the door unlocked I didn't see any harm in letting myself in." He wriggled his legs until he could use his shoulder to push himself up, and, wishing he was more graceful, managed to stand. "Your lads there decided to attack me before I had a chance to explain who I was." He glared at them threateningly. "And even after I told them, they still wanted to have a go."

"Oh, that won't do," the woman cried, shaking her head at the acolytes. "Untie him please, and return his staff – I assume that *is* your weapon, bailiff, yes? Oh, what a day this has been! First my husband, Henry, and now this."

John watched her as his wrists were untied, feeling terribly sorry for her. He'd only met Henry of Castellford a couple of times over the years, and hadn't realised he'd married this Holy Mother, whoever she was. He accepted his quarterstaff with a snarl at the man who'd hit him with it, and then found himself being escorted out of the front doors by the woman.

She was talking, telling him about her husband's suicide, and his terrible illness, and how their group was going to do God's work here in Northern England, and how sorry she was for his beating. And then he found himself in his horse's saddle, riding towards Wakefield, waving over his shoulder at the little, smiling woman.

CHAPTER FOUR

"And you just rode home?" Friar Tuck looked at him in surprise. "Without at least roughing up the pair who knocked you out? That's not like you, John, you must be getting old."

The bailiff simply shrugged and sipped at his ale with a bemused look on his bearded face. "It must have been the knock on the head that did it," he suggested. "Looking back now, it's like a dream. I just rode away without really questioning what was happening."

"You better watch that," Will Scaflock said. "We've seen people doing crazy things after a crack on the head. Although, in your case, I'm not sure anyone would notice."

John ignored his friends' good-natured laughter and rubbed at the back of his skull gingerly. "Nah, I've been fine in the days since. The lump's almost gone now too. If I have to go back to St Joseph's for anything again though, I'll be more careful. Those two that attacked me are still owed a few slaps."

The three friends nursed their drinks thoughtfully, enjoying the hubbub of voices and the warming, woody smell of the fire in the hearth of Wakefield's alehouse. There weren't many better places to be on an icy December evening, especially when you were there with men who'd shared so much with you over the years. They'd each saved one another's lives many times when part of Robin Hood's infamous, but much-loved, outlaw band, and, although all three were glad to have won their freedom, they still loved to share an ale and reminisce about old times.

Outside, the tavern-keeper, Alexander Gilbert, had hung sprigs of ivy over the door and shuttered windows, which contrasted with the snow and frost that covered the rest of the building. Inside, holly and mistletoe, with their shiny green leaves and bright red or white berries, seemed to sparkle in the flickering orange light of the fire.

"Soon be Christmas," Tuck noted happily, smiling as he thought of the coming feasts. Although he enjoyed his food and drink, and had the belly to show for it, he was still a formidable man whose grey cassock and tonsured head often made people underestimate him. "I wonder if they'll be celebrating much at St Joseph's. I doubt the Disciples of God care much about joyful occasions. They sound a serious bunch from what little gossip I've heard."

"They're bloody weird," Will growled. He was never one to mince his words, and Tuck cocked his head reprovingly.

"Just because they have slightly different ways of doing things," the friar said, "doesn't mean they're weird."

"Yes, it does," Will retorted, frowning. "That's exactly what it means."

John laughed at his friend's logic. "You're right, Scarlet. They're an odd lot and I doubt they'll be sharing a barrel of ale and a Christmas pie come the day. They'll be praying and…" He waved a meaty hand vaguely. "Doing whatever they get up to behind the doors of that church. We've all heard the rumours about odd sects and, well, odd sex!"

Tuck shook his head and glared at the bailiff. "Aye, rumours. Nothing more. You've been in the place and didn't see anything out of the ordinary."

"Apart from a dead body and a couple of monks that looked more like soldiers," Will grinned, flinching as Tuck made as if to hit him with the back of his hand.

"Henry of Castellford was the Holy Mother's husband; they had to bring him back for a Christian burial after he was found on the beach," the friar said. "Nothing strange about that. Well, it was a bit strange to be carrying him on a stretcher through the countryside like that, but you did say yourself, John, that the Holy Mother was very pleasant and friendly."

John, who had been smiling at the interplay between Tuck and Will, frowned again and stared into the fire. "She seemed to be," he agreed. "But there *was* something very strange about them, no matter what you say, Tuck. You should go along and visit them yourself and you'll see what I mean." His smile returned, taking in both of his friends. "Although, all you churchmen seem moon-touched to me."

Tuck had, of course, been a friar for many years, but even Will Scaflock had spent time as a monk once their gang had disbanded and they'd all struggled to come to terms with life as free men again. It hadn't quite worked out for Will, which perhaps wasn't surprising for a man who was commonly known as "Scarlet" thanks to his volatile temper, but it had certainly been a rewarding experience for him and led to him being a happier, more content individual now that he approached his mid-forties. Not that his tongue was any less sharp for all that.

"Moon-touched, perhaps. But neither of us would be stupid enough to go sneaking about a ruined old church on our own."

"Aye," John said sarcastically. "I should have known the members of a religious sect would try and kill an innocent visitor to their community. Silly me!"

"I'd try and kill you too," Scarlet retorted wryly. "If I found you wandering about my house."

"Did anything ever come of the trouble with Henry's children?" Tuck broke in. "You said there was talk of some issue with his will, John?"

The bailiff nodded and gestured for the innkeeper to bring another round of drinks. "Nothing happened with that," he said in reply to the friar's question. "Just another piece of gossip. It's a shame for Henry's son and daughter, to be left nothing but…If he wanted his new wife to get the lot, that's the way it goes. It's hardly the Lady's fault. Thank you, Alexander."

The purple-nosed innkeeper refilled the three companions' mugs from a foaming ale jug and gladly took the bailiff's coin as payment, before moving on to the patrons at the next table.

The door opened behind them and an icy wind preceded two tall young men who bustled inside and threw back grey hoods to reveal closely cropped hair and firm jawlines. Every eye in the place turned to look at them as one closed the door and the other rubbed his hands together to try and restore some warmth.

"That's the pair that knocked me out," John murmured, gently kicking Tuck and Will's feet beneath the table. "Disciples of God."

Perhaps back in their days in the greenwood Will would have made a joke about the men not looking very tough, but now he eyed them with silent interest. The taller, and younger of the two, apparently the leader, spoke to Alexander and then, receiving permission, turned to address the patrons of the alehouse.

"God grant you good evening, gentlemen of Wakefield," he said, but the impact of his words was somewhat hampered by a small voice in the corner.

"I'm a woman!"

Only a little put off by this remark, and the laughter that followed, the acolyte smiled thinly and continued. "Good men *and women* of Wakefield, I am Brother Colwin, and this is Brother David. We are from the Disciples of God. You may have heard of our group; we live and work near Altofts."

No one answered, which Colwin took as leave to continue. He noticed Little John, and there was a definite flicker of recognition in his eyes, but he never faltered, and his voice remained rich and strong.

"We will be having a celebration on the Ides of December—St Lucy's day—in the church you formerly knew as St Joseph's. There will be food and drink—"

"Is it free?" the small voice piped up again, but no one laughed this time, although they did all cheer when the acolyte confirmed the celebratory offerings would cost them nothing.

"What's the catch?" Alexander asked, put out by the thought of his customers spending an evening in Altofts instead of in his alehouse.

"No catch," Brother Colwin replied, looking around at everyone, even John, who was staring back balefully. "We just wish to offer a little charity to the local community at the joyous time of Christ's birth."

"I'll drink to that!" someone called out, raising his mug high and grinning as his words were echoed by others, even Alexander when Colwin told him to pour everyone another ale, paid for by the Disciples of God.

Only the bailiff and his two companions did not join in with the cheering, although none of them refused when Alexander brought his jug to their table once again.

For a moment, John thought Colwin and his silent, brooding companion might come over to the table and talk to them, but they must have known it would cause trouble and soon enough the tall acolyte paid the innkeeper for the round of drinks and then the pair left.

When the door closed behind them, shutting out the icy wind, and the fire had chased away the chill left in their wake, Will looked at John and rubbed at the stubble on his chin thoughtfully. "Honestly, I wouldn't really want to get in a fight with them."

John raised an eyebrow in mock disbelief. "Really?"

"Don't get me wrong," Scarlet said, nodding. "I'd take them, no doubt about that. Even if I am fifteen or twenty years older than them. But they look like they know how to handle themselves."

"They do," John muttered, ruefully rubbing the back of his head again. "What d'you think, Tuck? Do they look like men of God to you?"

The friar shrugged and lifted the drink Brother Colwin's silver had paid for. "You can't judge people by how they look, you should know that. Some of the most pleasant looking, apparently devout clergymen I've met have turned out to be sadistic, un-Christian fools." He took a long pull of ale and smacked his lips in satisfaction. "Those two young men might appear more like warriors than priests, but so did our old friend, Sir Richard-at-Lee, God rest his soul. I will be taking them up on their offer of meat and drink."

"There's a surprise," Will snorted. "It's lucky the devil didn't tempt you in the desert, Tuck. A mug of ale and the choice cuts from a suckling pig and you'd have been all his."

"That's enough of your sacrilege," the friar retorted indignantly, before his face softened again and he admitted, "I am partial to a bit of roast pork around Yuletide though. I hope they have some at St Joseph's."

John laughed humourlessly and stood up. "We'll find out in a couple of weeks," he said. "But for now, I'm away home to Amber. I need my bed."

"Do you want us to walk you home?" Will asked innocently. "Just in case the Disciples of God are waiting for you outside?"

Tuck made the sign of the cross at John's vicious reply and the friends bid one another good night.

A moment after the door had closed behind the giant bailiff, Tuck and Will shared a look and then they left too, clandestinely following John home. It wouldn't be the first time he'd been attacked after visiting an alehouse after all,[1] but they saw him safely indoors, heard the bolt being thrown across and the happy greeting he called to his wife and then, cursing the bitter cold, hurried to their own houses.

---

[1] See "The Escape"

CHAPTER FIVE

The days passed quickly for John, who always seemed to find winter a busy time as a bailiff. It made sense, he thought – when people were struggling to feed their families, they didn't prioritise things like paying fines for misdemeanours. Mind you, the people he dealt with never found it important to pay fines even in the height of summer, whether they were flush with money or not. And sometimes they were, for even highborn lords and ladies hated to part with their money and had to be persuaded on occasion.

"I wish I had more jobs like the one at Croftun Manor last winter," he said to Tuck as they were riding towards Altofts on the afternoon of the Disciples of God's Christmas celebration. "I really enjoyed that. Well," – he caught himself and looked a little guilty – "Maybe 'enjoyed' isn't the right word. It was a horrible situation there, but at least we were able to help Lady Isabella."

"Aye," the portly friar agreed. "It's satisfying when you solve a mystery and get justice for good people along the way."

Only the two of them were making the journey to St Joseph's. Will Scarlet had decided he wasn't interested in mingling again with 'a load of God-botherers' who, he suggested unkindly, probably flagellated themselves. Instead, Will was spending the evening with his new wife, Elspeth, and their infant son, Blase. He didn't have time to be riding around the countryside with his friends like he once did, and, since he seemed much happier than he ever had in all the time John had known him, John didn't push the matter.

"Will the place be busy, do you think?" Tuck asked fretfully. "I hope there's enough food to go around."

"Oh aye, they've invited all the surrounding townspeople," John said, then laughed at his friend's downcast expression. "I'm only joking. From what I've heard, they have indeed invited all the locals, but on different days. So, there'll be plenty to eat and drink, never fear."

Tuck's eyebrows lifted. "They must be rich if they can afford to feed so many people. I wonder where they get their money."

"Their Holy Mother, Alice de Staynton, will be wealthy enough, given what her husband bequeathed to her," John noted. "And, no doubt, they'll have the collections plate ready tonight, for any who wish to make a generous donation. You know how the Church works better than most, Tuck. They're never short of a coin or two."

The friar seemed unconvinced. "The Church as a whole is wealthy," he agreed. "But individual parishes are not necessarily. Besides, the Disciples of God are not part of the official Church, as far as I know. They're an unofficial group who'll be living by their own means."

John thought about that for a moment and then said, "You mean they're heretics?"

Tuck shook his head mildly. "Probably not. Who's to say what beliefs are heretical and what aren't? Maybe we'll get some idea of what they're doing tonight, but I wouldn't be quick to accuse anyone of that. Those charged with heresy can find themselves dead very easily, especially if they have a lot of money, or something else that some powerful man decides he'd like for himself."

John grunted in surprise. "What d'you mean?"

"Well," Tuck replied, raising his chin as he strove to remember an old tale he'd heard. "About a hundred or so years ago, in France, a young clerk in the service of a great archbishop took an interest in a young peasant girl. She rejected his advances, quite rightly, but the young man, knowing she held certain...unusual, yet quite harmless, religious beliefs, accused her of heresy."

"Bastard," Little John growled. He despised men who tried to force themselves on women.

"Quite," Tuck agreed. "But the girl was taken into custody and, under questioning by the archbishop, admitted that she had an instructress who lived in the city. This old lady was found and brought before the court where the churchmen demanded she renounce her heretical ways."

"Did she?"

Tuck shook his head emphatically. "Despite the pyre that had been setup, all ready to burn the unfortunate women, the old witch laughed at her interrogators, calling them foul names and uttering terrible blasphemies. Then she took out a ball of string from her tunic and threw it out of the window, shouting 'Catch!' to some invisible demon." The friar turned to gaze at John in wide-eyed amazement. "Then she was lifted aloft by unseen hands and pulled through the window after the ball of string." He clenched both fists, then opened them quickly, making a 'poof' sound as he did so. "She escaped, never to be seen again in France. Taken to safety, they said, by the same devils who'd once lifted Simon Magus into the air."

Little John rode on, digesting this bizarre tale in silence, and then he said, "So what happened to the young girl? Did she escape too?"

"Oh no, she was burned at the stake," Tuck said. "But she died in silence, refusing to cry out for mercy, like one of the martyrs of old, which much impressed those watching her ordeal. Many of them admitted they must have made a mistake with her after all."

John's face screwed up. "Oh well, that's all right then," he muttered caustically. "I'm sure that was a great comfort to her."

Just then St Joseph's came into sight and John was pleasantly surprised, for the place had been adorned with not only the usual evergreen foliage like holly and ivy, but with candles and rushlights. It was not at all windy, but it was cold, and clean white frost covered everything, showing up nicely against the cheery lights and winter decorations.

"At least they haven't hung any mistletoe," Tuck noted. "The Church frowns on that particular plant, sacred to the pagan druids as it was."

"So, they're *not* heretics then," John smiled. "Well, that's proof enough for me. No burnings at the stake here, eh?" He jumped down to the hard ground with a thud and tethered his horse to a post as Tuck followed his lead, breath steaming in the chill air. "Let's get drunk!"

The friar laughed and turned away to nod politely as more people from Wakefield walked past them towards the church doors with a cheery greeting. "I'd suggest we stay sober, unfortunately," he said to the bailiff when they were alone again. "After your last visit, it seems prudent to remain alert. Besides, I can't ride when I've had a few ales. I'd end up falling off and dying of the cold."

"All right then," John replied sadly. "Just four or five drinks. You keep your eyes open for anything out of the ordinary, though. Like, I don't know, upside down bibles or graven images of devils or that kind of thing."

"Agreed!"

They pushed open the double doors and went inside, struck immediately by the warmth and babble of sound which seemed to welcome them like an entity in its own right.

Their arrival was noticed immediately by the middle-aged, short woman who had spoken with John when he'd been knocked out on his last visit, and she headed straight for them, with a welcoming smile on her homely face.

"Holy Mother's coming," John muttered and Tuck, well trained from years as an outlaw, gave no indication that he'd heard.

"Bailiff! It's so good to see you fit and healthy." The Holy Mother touched John's arm as if they were old friends and he found himself returning her smile automatically. "And who have you brought with you? A wandering friar?"

Tuck bowed very slightly and introduced himself, which drew an exclamation of delight from Lady Alice.

"The famous Friar Tuck, here, in our community? God be praised, I've heard so much about you and your fine work on the Lord's behalf, helping the poor and downtrodden to stand against their oppressors. But," – she gazed up at John towering over them and narrowed her eyes – "that must mean that you are Little John. Oh, how wonderful!"

Both men were used to being treated as if they were special since their fame had spread far and wide over the years and, usually, it meant little to them. For some reason, both John and Tuck were grinning at the Holy Mother now, as if her personal approval was something they'd always sought after.

"I suppose I should talk with the others who've made the journey here from your village," she said, and it was as if the idea was anathema to her, as if she wished she could spend every moment of the evening in the company of these two legendary figures. "Please enjoy the food and drink we've laid out for you, and, in a little while, I shall tell you all about the Disciples of God, and what our mission is here in England. Merry Christmas, my friends!"

"Thank you, my lady," Tuck said, bowing again, as he might have done to one of his own Franciscan bishops.

"Oh, please call me Holy Mother," she replied, smiling brightly. "Everyone does."

With that she was swallowed up by the other villagers from Wakefield – almost thirty of them had walked or ridden there that evening – and bailiff and friar were left standing until, eventually, someone jostled Tuck and, in the ensuing apologies, both he and John somehow ended up with a mug of ale in their hands.

"What do you make of her?"

The friar's eyes followed Lady Alice as she moved about the room but the smile no longer lingered on his face. Instead he looked serious, and a little uncertain. "She's…"

"Striking?" John offered. "Charming? Friendly?"

"All of those things," Tuck agreed thoughtfully. "But also rather overwhelming. Which is only to be expected, I suppose." He watched the people Lady Alice left in her wake as she walked from person to person within the pew-less church, noting their reactions. "Leaders of sects like this are always charismatic – it's how they draw followers to them."

"You think we can trust her?"

Tuck gestured vaguely with his hand. "What is there to trust? We're not joining her group. I'm very interested to know what their teachings are though, for a holy woman like that could be a powerful force for good around Altofts."

"And them?"

Tuck looked at the two young acolytes that had come to the alehouse in Wakefield with the invitation to this celebration. Brother Colwin, the younger of the pair, nodded beatifically at the guests as they passed by, reminding Tuck of a Templar or Hospitaller Knight with his aloof, pious demeanour. Brother David followed behind him as usual, smiling occasionally although his expression darkened when he looked at the bailiff.

"They certainly take themselves very seriously," the friar noted lightly.

A table had been piled with food and it made John's mouth water even before he had a chance to taste it. Pies with perfectly baked crusts, sweetmeats, cake, freshly baked bread – it wasn't exactly a feast fit for a king, but it looked and smelled divine, and was probably the best meal most of the men and women from Wakefield would eat the entire winter. And all washed down with not only ale, but wine too.

It seemed the Disciples of God wanted to make a good impression on the people who lived nearby and, thus far, it was working perfectly.

The gathering was a very relaxed affair, since most of the people there knew one another quite well, living in the same village as they did. The members of the new sect were warm and friendly and smiled rather more than John was used to, which made him mutter irritably in Tuck's ear. The friar merely laughed and told him to enjoy the free food.

Once the participants were suitably 'refreshed', Lady Alice stood in the chancel and looked out at them all, waiting patiently until her silent, beatific presence was noted and a respectful yet curious silence fell.

"Thank you, friends," she said at last, beaming around at them all. John noticed that most of the other Disciples of God remained within the gathered group of villagers, but Brother Colwin and Brother David now stood with arms folded against opposite walls of the old church, watching the people, rather than their leader.

"You think they're expecting trouble?" the bailiff whispered to Tuck.

"Can't blame them for being careful," the friar replied softly. "You never know what might happen when you give a room full of people drink, then expect them to listen to a sermon on what might be heresy."

"Sshhh," a woman behind them hissed and Tuck fell silent, smirking at Little John like a misbehaving child but not fancying his chances in an argument with Agnes, the sharp-tongued Wakefield butcher's wife who had arms bigger than her husband's hams.

"You are all *most* welcome here in St Joseph's," the Holy Mother went on, her voice rich and clear, and stronger than her appearance would suggest. "We invited you here, first, to celebrate the joyous occasion of Christ's birth, second, to let you all see what we've done with this old building that was previously falling to sad ruin, and third, I wanted to let you know a little about our mission here."

There was some fidgeting but the audience waiting politely enough for her to continue. John could see most of the people were bored already, however, and wanted nothing more than to get as much free food and drink down their necks before it was time to head home. The Lady's next words caused a ripple of surprised interest, though.

"The Disciples of God exist to fight what we call the Black Lords." The Holy Mother gazed around at the villagers, who appeared bemused but curious at this strange pronouncement.

"Black Lords?" Tuck asked, trying to keep his voice as neutral as possible and wondering if the outlandish term was just another way of talking about the same old evil forces Christianity had battled for hundreds of years. Apparently not.

"The Black Lords," replied Lady Alice clearly, "are a new threat to our souls. Satan has grown much stronger in England thanks to the recent troubles with famines and wars and other wickedness. You've all seen evidence of this."

Some of the villagers nodded enthusiastically at her words, for they'd suffered plenty of injustice and hardship during their lives and it always seemed like things had been easier during past times. So the older folk claimed at least, and it wasn't hard to believe.

The Holy Mother reached down to her belt and drew forth a knife, holding it up for all to see. It was a long, finely crafted weapon but looked vaguely sinister in the hand of the middle-aged, pleasant woman at the lectern. "We fight the Black Lords with whatever weapons we have, consecrated to be effective against those who occupy the spirit realm."

John looked at Tuck and saw amazement on the friar's round face. Fighting demons with real blades? What madness was this?

"What if you can't afford a fancy knife like that?" someone asked.

"No matter," said the Holy Mother, nodding reassuringly. "The quality of the material in our earthly realm is not the most important thing. You can fight the Black Lords with nothing more than a length of sharpened oak, as long as it is properly blessed and given the correct, protective blessing."

"If these demons occupy the spirit realm," Tuck asked. "Are they invisible? And, if so, how does one fight them with earthly weapons?"

"These are skills that must be learned, brother friar," admitted the Lady Alice. "Not everyone can do it, it must be said. Only those with certain natural abilities can stand against the Black Lords."

Little John eyed the villagers, most of whom looked bored again. All this talk of fighting demons was of little interest to them and, judging by the frowns on a few faces, some of the people were beginning to think the Disciples of God were moon-touched. The promise of more ale was enough to maintain the respectful ambience though, and the Holy Mother went on, perhaps realising the crowd's good will would only last for so long.

"We have certain holy relics here in St Joseph's which draw the Black Lords to us, keeping their baleful influence away from the surrounding towns and villages, like Wakefield. Or at least, that is our hope, once we are truly settled here and can properly begin our Great Work."

Patrick Prudhomme, the village headman, spoke up now, from the very front of the crowd. "This is all very well, and we greatly appreciate the repast you've put on for us but…" He looked slightly embarrassed but forged on, putting his concerns into words. "Are we going to have the Church coming to Wakefield and causing trouble over all this? Abbott Ness and Archbishop Melton don't really like, er…change," he finished rather lamely.

Lady Alice beamed at him and spread her hands wide. "I foresee no trouble with the Church, my friend. We are not preaching against their teachings, not at all. We are just trying to take the fight against evil directly to Satan and his Black Lords. If anything, I would hope the Archbishop will approve of our work here."

That seemed to ease Patrick's mind, and he nodded in response to her words.

"I've said enough for now, I don't want to bore you," the Holy Mother said with a laugh. "Thank you for listening. Now, please eat and drink your fill and if you have any questions about our group or our work here, I will be happy to answer them. Of course, we still have much to do to return this wonderful old building to its former glory so, if you have a coin to spare, please drop it in the plates carried by Brothers Colwin and David." She gestured at the young acolytes standing by the walls. "God bless you, friends, and may He protect you against the Black Lords. Merry Christmas, all!"

Almost instantly, the people broke into conversation amongst themselves, discussing the Holy Mother's words, Satan's unseen servants, and, more commonly, whether the bird pie was any good or if the crust was a bit burnt. John found the chatter quite amusing – he hadn't really thought the folk of Wakefield would take the Disciples of God's professed mission too seriously – but Tuck didn't think any of this was a joke.

"I'm all for it," he said, when the bailiff asked him why he looked so dour. "This sect standing against the forces of evil, I mean. The more people trying to do good in the world, the better. Do I really believe they battle actual denizens of hell with sharpened sticks?" He shrugged noncommittally. "Who knows? Does it matter? If it leads to the acolytes living in accordance with the bible, that's what matters. And I have to agree," he looked up at John. "This crust is a tad burnt."

"Won't stop you wolfing it down like a starving man though," the bailiff retorted, helping himself to a large section of the pie in question. When he turned back to Tuck, he saw the friar was engaged in conversation with some of the villagers, who were asking for his opinion on this odd new sect. So, John ate in silence, watching the Holy Mother as she moved about the room, smiling the whole time, answering questions and spreading Christmas cheer everywhere she went.

The woman was a good judge of character, for she avoided the people that John knew from personal experience would be the least interested in the Disciples of God. Although it was quite obvious on the faces of some of them – drunken disdain and disinterest was easy to spot after all – the Holy Mother avoided even those whose expressions were neutral, somehow sensing they would not care to join in her Great Work.

It appeared to be certain types who were drawn to her with earnest looks and eager questions: widows and widowers; those who'd suffered some personal tragedy recently; younger folk who hadn't yet found their place in the world; men who found Lady Alice physically alluring, of which there were more than John would have expected. He looked on with great interest as the various people spoke with the Holy Mother and wondered just how many new recruits the

Disciples of God would have after this meeting. Three or four, with perhaps one or two being truly devoted to the sect, at least for a while? His eyes came to rest on the shaven-headed figure of Brother Colwin, who was staring back at him with something of a malevolent cast to his expression and, for a moment, John, never a subtle man, was sorely tempted to stalk across to the young acolyte and pin him against the wall.

"When are you planning on heading home?" Tuck was by his side again, empty handed yet apparently satiated for a while.

"Now, if you're ready," John replied. "I won't be joining the fight against the Black Lords, and I can't see you battling invisible enemies with that trusty cudgel you keep hidden inside your cassock, so we may as well be off."

"All right. We'll thank Lady Alice for her hospitality first, come on."

They began walking towards the Holy Mother, John still giving Brother Colwin a look that almost invited the younger man to come and finish the fight they'd started here days earlier. Before they could push past the villagers crammed within St Joseph's however, a voice cried out over the hubbub, loud and clear and almost hysterical.

"He's dead! Someone, help me – I think he's dead!"

CHAPTER SIX

Both John and Tuck reacted to the cry immediately, running towards the distraught woman at the door leading into the vestry in which John had previously been knocked unconscious. Before they could make it there, however, Brother Colwin appeared, barring their way.

"What are you doing, you fool?" John demanded. "The friar here is a healer. He can help whoever's in trouble in there."

"We can deal with it ourselves," the acolyte replied coldly, and he seemed unflustered by the shocking turn of events.

"Let them in, for God's sake," cried the woman who'd shouted for aid in the first place. "It's Brother Morris – maybe he's not dead, maybe he just looked like he was. Let the friar in, Brother Colwin!"

Again, the shaven-headed young man shook his head. "The Disciples of God will see to their own troubles. The friar's aid is not required, and you, bailiff," he glared at John, "have no official powers here."

"Is that right?" Little John drew himself up to his full height, towering almost a full head above even Colwin, who was not a small man. "I'm a representative of the sheriff. Of the king. The last thing you people want is to draw their attention to yourselves, trust me. Now…" He reached out and grabbed the acolyte by the arm, spinning him so that, somehow, Colwin ended up kneeling on the floor, trapped in a headlock he had no chance of escaping from. Brother David was pushing his way towards them from the other side of the room however, ready to help his fellow acolyte.

"That's enough of this foolishness!" The Holy Mother's voice cut through the excited uproar like a war-arrow through flesh and the people hastily parted to let her through. She strode up to the vestry door, shaking her head in exasperation. "Enough I say, Colwin. We have nothing to hide and, like the bailiff says, perhaps Friar Tuck can be of assistance. Let them pass."

"Aye," John growled, taking the opportunity to rub his knuckles painfully on the back of Colwin's skull. "Let us pass, lad, before I—"

"Bailiff! Enough."

John let go of the acolyte, whose face was scarlet from lack of air and embarrassment. Before he could say anything though, Tuck was past him and John hurriedly followed.

A man lay slumped over the candlelit desk in the corner. He had a ring of straggly greying hair beneath a bald pate, looked about forty-five, and was very clearly deceased.

"Damn it!" John shouted. "If there was any hope of helping him, that idiot at the door—"

"Forget it," Tuck said, patting the bailiff's arm as if he was soothing a dog with its hackles up. "This fellow's been dead for a while. Look at the colour of his skin."

They could hear the Holy Mother ordering Colwin and David to marshal the villagers out of the church and on their way home. She was telling the people to take some food with them, to offset any irritation they might have felt at not being allowed to see the dead man – an exciting event at any time after all, never mind during a Christmas feast within the home of a strange new religious sect.

"Any evidence of violence?" Tuck muttered as he and John examined the corpse and the room about them in the wan, flickering light from the single candle on the desk.

"Doesn't seem to be. No signs of a struggle, no apparent wounds or injuries on him, no discarded weapons…"

"What's killed him then?" The friar eyed the dead man curiously. "He looks far too young to have died from old age as he sat here."

The Holy Mother came into the room and exclaimed in shock at the sad sight before her. "Brother Morris," she whispered from behind the hand that sought to mask her grief. "How?"

"Here, Lady Alice." Tuck lifted a second chair from the other side of the desk and placed it behind the Holy Mother, gently guiding her down onto it. "It looks like he maybe had a fit or something. It's not all that uncommon and, if it's any comfort, he probably didn't suffer for long."

"Oh, God," the woman said softly, tears streaking her cheeks as she looked at the dead man, as if wishing him to get up and come to life again. "First my poor Henry, and now this, it's unbearable."

There was a cup of ale on the desk beside the dead man's hand and John lifted it now, peering into the dark liquid and sniffing it. His nose wrinkled and he passed it to the friar with a frown. "What d'you make of this?"

Tuck sniffed the drink and grimaced. "Smells like mouse piss. Hemlock would be my guess," he said. "Seems we have our cause of death." He looked at Lady Alice, as if he would ask her something, but her distress was plain and he turned his attention back to the desk. "What's that?" he said to John. "Under his hand there."

Carefully, the bailiff lifted Brother Morris's limp right hand and drew out what Tuck was asking for. It was a piece of parchment and, now that it had been pointed out to him, John could see a pot of ink and a quill pen on the desk too. He handed the parchment to his friend, noticing the Latin letters written on it and knowing Tuck would be able to read them easier than he might.

"What does it say?" the Holy Mother asked fretfully. "Does it have anything to do with his…" She choked off a sob and looked away from the body. "His death."

Tuck's eyes scanned the writing in the gloom, but even John couldn't tell what he was thinking from the changing expressions on his face.

"He killed himself," the friar said at last. "He mixed hemlock, as I thought, with his ale and drank it down." He scanned further down the parchment, frowning in concentration. "His writing is shaky, as if, perhaps, he wrote this after taking the concoction. There is a will, however." He glanced up at Lady Alice and found her staring at him from red-rimmed eyes, but she said nothing, simply waited for him to continue. "Was he—"

"Brother Morris," the lady offered.

"Was Brother Morris a wealthy man? I'm not sure if I'm reading this correctly."

The Holy Mother frowned. "I couldn't say. Wealth is not something we discuss here. But he lived simply, as we all do."

"He has left all he owned to you, and the Disciples of God," Tuck said, watching for her reaction, but her expression didn't waver. He held the document out to her. "If I am reading the figures correctly, your sect is now rather better off than you were a few hours ago."

Lady Alice took the proffered suicide note in a shaky hand but placed it on the table without reading it as another sob wracked her body. Tuck led John out of the room with quiet words of condolence for the Holy Mother and promises to pray for the dead man's soul. They passed Brothers Colwin and David, glowering at them in silence, and went out into the cold night.

Neither man said another word until they were safely in the saddle and well away from St Joseph's.

"Why pray for his soul?" Little John wondered as they cantered along the road, breath misting behind them in the moonlight. "I thought taking your own life meant you went straight to hell."

Tuck nodded and there was a deeply troubled look on his face. "The note left behind by that acolyte was…disturbing," he said. "The fellow seemed to think..." He trailed off and sighed heavily although it was lost in the rumble of cantering hooves and the biting December chill that swirled about them. "I must think on the poor man's words before I can even begin to understand what was going through his head before he drank that terrible mixture."

The rest of the journey was made in silence, even when they passed others on their way back, on foot, to Wakefield. Little John was glad to get indoors and take his wife in his arms that night, for the frost was settling thickly across the land, and seeing a corpse was always a stark reminder of one's own mortality.

CHAPTER SEVEN

"There's something not right with the Disciples of God."

Little John raised his eyebrows at Tuck's pronouncement when they bumped into one another in the village the next morning and snorted humourlessly. "Your famed intuition hasn't deserted you yet, I see," he replied.

The friar waved a hand irritably, wandering away from the row of houses and shops so their words wouldn't be overheard. Although it was early and the sun hadn't yet risen to burn away the frost and mist, people were already up and about their business. No doubt many of them had spent a fitful, sleepless night after the excitement at St Joseph's, Tuck included. He'd lain awake, going over the contents of the dead acolyte's last will and testament in his mind and growing ever more certain that something was wrong.

"I mean it, John. That sect, despite their pronouncements of battling evil and doing God's work, are going to cause trouble for a lot of people. I can feel it."

John nodded. "Aye, I already had my suspicions before last night. Colwin and David are no simple disciples of Christ – they're guards, and they're there to make sure no-one gets close enough to find out what's really going on. You saw Colwin trying to stop us seeing what had happened in the vestry. He wanted to cover it up before anyone discovered the truth."

Tuck didn't say anything for a while, until John asked him what had been written in the dead man's letter.

"He seemed to believe that his suicide would not be a sin."

John frowned. "Just like Henry of Castellford."

"Brother Morris's letter suggested he'd discussed it with someone else in the Disciples of God. He believed he could end his life but, instead of going straight to hell for his sin, he would be taken up by God to fight against the Black Lords."

"And what do you believe, old friend?"

Tuck's lip curled in a sneer. "I believe someone wanted whatever money Brother Morris had, and persuaded him to take his life that they might get their hands on it."

"Brother Colwin," John growled. "That's why he tried to stop us going into the room – he didn't want us to see the letter because he feared we'd figure it out. Damn him! What are we going to do, Tuck?"

They stopped by a fence, resting their arms upon the damp wood and gazing into the field at the cattle, light frost settling upon them as they pondered the situation.

"There's nothing really we can do," Tuck said eventually. "We have no proof any crime's been committed."

"No proof?" the bailiff exclaimed. "Two members of the Disciples of God have taken their own lives in the past month or so! What more evidence can possibly be needed?"

"As far as we know," Tuck said evenly, "both men committed the act voluntarily. They were not murdered. Madness, or gullibility perhaps, is not a crime."

"We just do nothing then?" John slammed a great fist on the fence, sending vibrations all the way along it and drawing a scowl from Tuck who felt the shockwave going up his arms.

"It would be useful to know why Lady Alice's husband decided to throw himself off that cliff," the friar replied with a reproving stare. "Next time the sheriff gives you a job to do near the coast, you could maybe ask about in Newsham and see if anyone knows anything. Other than that? Our hands are tied and it's really none of our business anyway. Brother Colwin knows we read the letter so I expect he'll keep his head down and there'll be no more suicides connected to St Joseph's. For a while anyway."

Again, they stood together in silence, pondering the strange new religious sect that had come into the lives of the people of Yorkshire and how much they might be trusted.

"What makes intelligent people fall for these things, Tuck?" the bailiff asked sadly.

"We all have needs, John," came the reply. "As incredible as it might seem to us, certain people enjoy the feeling of brotherhood and camaraderie they get from a religious order like the Disciples." He shrugged. "Remember our time as outlaws and the bonds we all formed then. Closer than family. Besides," he smiled. "At one time the Romans thought *all* Christians were mad. Perhaps in a thousand years everyone will be battling Black Lords and remembering the Lady Alice as a great prophet."

John returned his friend's smile, thinking back to their time on the opposite side of the law in the greenwood. A horrible, frightening existence, where death lurked around every tree trunk and yet, some of his happiest memories were of those days and, undoubtedly, the greatest friends he'd ever have were met then: Tuck, Will Scarlet, Much, Marjorie and, of course, Robert Hood himself.

"Right, enough nostalgia," the bailiff said, drawing himself up and patting Tuck on the arm affectionately. "I have work to do today. Unfortunately to the south, not over on the coast at Newsham. But next time I'm near there, I'll see what I can find out about Henry of Castellford, all right?"

"Try and be discreet about it," Tuck said, before he remembered who he was talking to and how hard it was for a man almost seven feet tall to be subtle. "Well, at least try not to get into too many fights."

"You know me," John laughed, and they went on their separate ways, both grinning, both glad to be alive.

PART TWO – SPRING 1330

CHAPTER EIGHT

As it turned out, Little John was too busy to worry about the Disciples of God or the Holy Mother's dead husband, as the sheriff, Sir Henry, did not see winter as a time for resting, despite the roads becoming treacherous due to the weather. The bailiff was constantly travelling from village to town around Yorkshire and, in fact, was often accompanied by one or two of the sheriff's soldiers nowadays. There had been an increasing tendency for people to refuse to pay their lawful fines and often they would get violent, which that was never a good tactic when facing Little John. One man in Peniston had ended up with a broken jaw, while another in Kirklees would never breathe properly again, and a third was unlikely to father children any time soon given the force of the kick the bailiff had placed between his legs.

When he'd started this job, John was well known as a vicious outlaw himself, and his reputation, along with his great size, had been enough to make folk think twice about attacking him.

Now, a few years after Robin Hood's apparent death, and the disbanding of his gang, people were beginning to forget about the likes of Little John. Life was hard, and memories were short, especially when it came to handing over money to someone you didn't want to give it to, like a bailiff. And John was, despite his appearance and fearsome reputation, not a man who enjoyed hurting people, so he was glad when spring returned and his workload seemed to ease. Perhaps Sir Henry had noticed the bailiff's increasing dissatisfaction with the work and given him less as a result.

It was a strange relationship between them: the sheriff respected John and knew he was a very wealthy man in his own right, having 'earned' a lot of money during his time as an outlaw. All of Hood's gang, Tuck and Will Scaflock included, were in the same position of being financially well off and not really needing regular employment as a result. It wasn't in their nature to live a life of ease though, which was why the sheriff, recognising John's exceptional talents, had given him a job as a roving bailiff. John had always been a champion for the little man, and a supporter of justice, which was what had seen him become an outlaw in the first place, so he'd been happy to go around the county gathering unpaid fines from people who'd committed crimes against their compatriots.

As the daffodils' pale yellow petals burst into full bloom however, the sheriff eased John's workload and the bailiff was glad of it. There had been no further strange deaths or reports of any trouble from, or about, the Disciples of God, who seemed to be battling the Black Lords quietly enough from within the fully refurbished St Joseph's and the urgency John and Tuck had once felt to investigate the suicides had abated along with the winter snows.

When the sheriff sent a letter asking John to collect a fine from a particularly unpleasant individual in Bainton, not far from the eastern coast, he remembered Lady Alice's husband, and his fall from the cliffs near there. It was the perfect opportunity to pay a visit to the village of Newsham and find out if any of the locals knew about the suicide.

He waved goodbye to Amber and set off on a dry, crisp morning that promised to be mostly dry. He carried enough food and drink to last him a few days, although both the places he planned on visiting were on the main road. That meant he would be able to buy provisions easily enough, and also, hopefully, avoid any robbers, most of whom would stick to quieter backroads and look for easier prey.

Although it was almost sixty miles to Bainton, John made good time for the roads were clear after the winter and he was finally becoming a better rider thanks to all the hours he spent on horseback these days. The job there proved easier than he'd feared too – the troublesome man he'd been sent to collect the fine from turned out to be older than the sheriff's records suggested and he hadn't given the bailiff any trouble, handing over the coins without argument.

John spent the night on a bench in Bainton's alehouse, enjoying an evening of local sing-song, banter and stories, along with a hearty stew and a couple of fresh, strong ales for just a few coins. then, the next day, just four days since leaving Wakefield, he rode into Newsham.

The air here was bracing, being situated so close to the sea, and the first thing John did was ride to see the cliffs Henry of Castellford had thrown himself from.

He tethered his horse to a bush and stood, looking out over the water in silence, listening to the cries of the birds and the gentle sounds of the waves, and breathing deeply of the invigorating air. It was a peaceful place, full of nature's beauty, which only made it more poignant to think of the man who felt he couldn't continue living any longer, and had decided instead to fall from here onto the rocks far beneath.

The bailiff didn't particularly like heights and, peering over the edge to the beach more than three hundred feet below, he felt slightly dizzy and wondered at the mindset of any man who could end his life in such a manner. What had been so terrible that Henry could not go on any longer, despite being a Christian and knowing suicide was a terrible sin? John hoped to get some answers from the people of Newsham and he headed there now.

"Well, you're a big lad aren't you?"

John smiled politely at the woman's comment and the suggestive wink which set her two companions laughing. He'd just ridden into the village and these three were the first people he'd come across so, judging them as good a source of information as any, and probably better than most given how the conversation had started, he jumped down from the saddle and stood before the ladies, trying to smooth his unkempt beard and wild, long hair.

The one who'd spoken to him was middle-aged, but her years didn't weigh heavily on her for her face was unlined and pleasant. The other two were around twenty and, from the looks of them, probably the older woman's children.

"God give you good day, ladies," John said. "I'm a visitor—"

"Obviously," the older woman interjected. "There's only a few people live in this village. I think we'd have noticed you wandering about the place if you hailed from here."

"I suppose so," he grinned. "You're right – I'm from Wakefield. I was wondering if you knew the man who jumped off the cliffs not so long ago? Henry of Castellford was his name; I believe he was from here originally, before being granted land near Pontefract."

The smiles fell from the women's faces and one of the younger ones muttered something John couldn't quite make out.

"You two go on ahead," the older one said, in a tone that brooked no argument. "I'll be along shortly."

Without reply the pair wandered off and John waited until they were lost from sight behind one of the small houses set a little back from the road. "Your daughters?" he asked. "They look a lot like you."

The woman's face split in a wide grin and she laughed. "Daughters? Oh, you are a flatterer. They're my grandchildren. I had their mother when I was fifteen."

"Oh, really?" John wasn't interested in flirting with her, the compliment had been entirely accidental, but it was always good to bring people onto your side if you wanted information from them. "You only look about thirty," he said.

She laughed again, but then her happy expression faded as she looked at him. "You wanted to know about Henry?"

He decided to be as honest as possible without mentioning the Disciples of God. Who knew what influence they might hold in this remote place after all? "I'm a bailiff," he admitted. "I wondered if anyone knew why Henry had killed himself."

"He wasn't very well," she said, shrugging. "That's what he wrote in the letter he left behind. He thought he was dying."

"He *thought* he was dying? You don't sound convinced."

"I barely knew him," the woman admitted. "But I saw him that week and he looked as fit and healthy as any man his age. He was tall – not as big as you, but a big man nonetheless – and broad and strong. But I'm not a barber-surgeon, what do I know?"

"Look," he said levelly. "I'm not here to cause trouble for anyone. Like you, I wondered if that story about him being ill was maybe not true. If you know anything more about it, please tell me."

She gazed up at him, as if gauging his sincerity, and then nodded decisively. "All right. You look dangerous, but there's something kind about your face. I'll trust you, even though I have no idea who you are." She started walking along the road, away from him. "Come on," she called back over her shoulder. "Follow me. But if you're lying, and here to cause trouble, may God smite you right in the bollocks."

John blinked at her odd turn of phrase, shook his head in amusement, and strode after her, wondering just what he was getting himself into.

"What about my horse?"

"It'll be fine tethered there, don't fret. No-one will steal it."

Newsham was only a small place so it didn't take long for them to reach their destination: a house with a very well-maintained thatched roof and windows facing towards the sea. The woman knocked on the door. "Elspeth! Elspeth, it's Marion from along the road. I've got a visitor for you."

There was a sound from within and then the door was opened by a small, narrow-faced woman who smiled at her caller and then frowned in alarm at the sight of the giant, bearded man on her threshold.

"Who the hell's he?"

John's companion smiled reassuringly. "Bailiff from Wakefield. He's looking into your da's death." She squeezed John's arm. "He seems all right, so I thought you might want to speak with him."

"Looking into my father's so-called 'suicide' are you?" Elspeth demanded, stepping back from the doorway to allow John inside. "About damn time. Come on then, let's hear what you have to say."

The bailiff bent his head – he was much too tall to fit under most doors – and went inside, finding a cosy fire which seemed to be keeping the single roomed house warm despite the windows being un-shuttered.

The woman who'd brought him there said farewell and went off about her own business, while Elspeth closed the door and placed another small log onto the hearth, poking it into even brighter life and stirring something which smelled delightfully meaty in the pot above it.

"Sit there, while I get us something to drink," she said, fetching two wooden cups and filling them with a liquid which John soon discovered was a rather pleasant watered wine. Then she sat at the table which seemed tiny next to John's great bulk. "So, what makes you think there's something not right about my father's death?"

He opened his mouth to tell her some of the things that had happened since Henry of Castellford had jumped from the nearby cliffs but, before he could say a word, Elspeth spoke again.

"You know that me and my brother were left nothing in his will?"

She was clearly indignant, and John could see it would be most instructive just to let her say her piece. He doubted he could stop her anyway, for she had clearly been thinking about this for months.

"That bitch, Alice, turned his head and made him believe…strange things. Things most people would think mad. Have you met her? What did you make of her, eh?" Elspeth didn't allow John to reply, indeed she barely paused for a breath, continuing her tirade as the bailiff listened intently. "Disciples? They're mad. All they wanted was my father's money. The Lady made him think she loved him. You've seen her, did you think her beautiful? She's short and dumpy and no great looker, yet somehow she managed to win over my da. And I hear she's remarried already, before he's even cold in the grave she put him in! How does she do it? Black Lords? Pfft, I think *she*'s the real evil. Her and those bloody Disciples of God. She used my father's influence to get that church over your way, St Joseph's aye, that's the one, and then someone made him kill himself to get his money. There, what have you to say now, bailiff?"

For a time, John had nothing to say at all. He sat, sipping his wine and digesting Elspeth's tirade, believing it was nothing more than the bitter ramblings of someone who felt they'd been robbed of their rightful inheritance. And then he remembered one thing in particular that she'd said and looked at her curiously. "Lady Alice has already remarried?"

"So I heard," Elspeth said venomously. "Some old fellow, another member of that moon-touched sect of hers."

This was news to John, and he vowed to find out more on his return home. For now, he had other questions for the red-faced woman. "Did the coroner or the local bailiff not look into your father's death?"

She scowled derisively. "Oh, they looked into it. They read the letter he was forced to write, and the will he left behind giving everything to her, and they decided everything was all right. God take them, they couldn't be bothered to do their bloody jobs."

"Your father killed himself," John said softly. "Because he had an illness, is that right?"

"That's what he wrote in his letter," Elspeth agreed frostily. "He'd been told by some barber-surgeon that he had a wasting disease that would kill him slowly and painfully."

"Did you meet the surgeon yourself?"

"Of course not," the woman retorted. "I'd have sent the fool on his way. There was nothing wrong with my father, anyone could see that. A few headaches now and again, nothing terrible."

"Do you know who the surgeon was?" John asked, hoping he might be able to locate the man and question him about the diagnosis, but Elspeth was shaking her head.

"No idea, it was one of those big Disciples with the shaved heads who hired him. My father described him to me when I asked, but I didn't recognise the fellow: A tall, slim man with a scar below his eye, apparently."

John met her furious gaze and, although he expected to be berated for it, asked her the question he'd been wanting an answer to all the time he'd been in Elspeth's house. "Do you have any evidence that the Disciples of God did anything against the law?"

To his surprise, there was no explosion of anger in response, only a frustrated sigh. "No. But I know my father. I know that he started having headaches and spells of disorientation from the moment he joined that sect, and I know he was manipulated into leaving us, his children, out of his will in order to grant everything to them."

"But, unless I'm mistaken," he replied, "you, as the second, female, child wouldn't have inherited anything anyway." He was referring to the law of primogeniture, where land would be passed down, undivided, to the first-born male child of the dead person.

Elspeth nodded. "You're correct. My brother, Nigel, was to be granted the lands near Pontefract. But my father had other valuable things – weapons, household items, books, and other things of that nature – which he'd always said would be left to me." She looked around at her small house sadly. "It wasn't much, compared to the lands in Castellford, but it would have made my family's life that bit easier." Her eyes blazed as she turned back to John and slammed a hand on the table, making the wine jug jump. "And it was *mine*! Not theirs, mine!"

They looked at one another in silence for a while, the warmth in the room and the watered wine doing their part to calm Elspeth until, eventually, she shook her head and spoke again, this time in a more level voice. "My father changed when he joined the Disciples of God, and when he married *Lady* Alice." The epithet was dripping with venom. "We were a close family, bailiff, until then. They're all tools of the devil, and people like you will eventually find that out!"

There wasn't much to be said after that. Elspeth's ire faded now that she'd said her piece and, with John's reassurance that he would look into things if he could, they parted ways and the bailiff walked back to his horse, thoughts like hammers in his head as he tried to figure out what, if anything, the Disciples of God might really be up to.

It did not make sense to John, who, although he didn't like Colwin, wasn't convinced the man was terrifying enough to scare two men into suicide, essentially. Or perhaps John just couldn't see it because he himself was not intimidated by the shaven-headed acolyte…

He took an apple from his horse's saddlebag and allowed the animal to take it from his hand, while he stroked its mane and spoke cheerfully to it. He'd never been particularly comfortable with horses, but this one had been a loyal companion on his many travels and appeared happy to see him. It was always a nice feeling to be well received by a friend after listening to so much anger and bitterness and John was glad to mount up and head back towards Wakefield.

Perhaps, in the four days it took him to reach home, he might come up with an idea of what the Disciples of God were all about, and what, if anything, he should do about it.

And perhaps his horse would sprout wings and fly to Wakefield, he thought humourlessly.

CHAPTER NINE

When Tuck had been pardoned for his crimes along with the rest of Robin Hood's old gang, the friar had come to live in Wakefield. The priest in St Mary's, Father Myrc, was a friend to the outlaws and offered to put Tuck up since, although the law was no longer after him, certain powerful churchmen had not forgiven him for his actions against them. Time had passed since then, three years in fact, and the men who'd been after Tuck had died or forgotten about him so, although he could have probably returned to his old home with the Franciscans in Lewes Priory, he simply did not want to.

He enjoyed living here in Wakefield – the villagers liked him and often came to him for advice, and he had many friends here even apart from Little John and Will Scarlet. So, here he would remain, in the little house he'd built just outside the grounds of St Mary's until he had a reason to move on.

One of the tasks he still did in return for Father Myrc's early kindness and protection was to make sure the church grounds were kept neat and in good repair. He had been a wrestler in his youth and was still sturdy and strong, so he was happy to mend storm-damaged storehouses and fences and sweep leaves into piles for, as he said, it was all God's work, and kept him fit. Of course, John and Will would laugh at that and point to Tuck's belly but, despite his love of food and drink, the friar was a match for most men if it came to a fight.

He was replacing a rotten doorframe on the back of St Mary's that morning, sweating thanks to the spring sunshine and the wood, which wouldn't come away in large pieces. Instead, he was forced to hammer away at it, as it just crumpled under his blows, meaning the job was taking longer than he'd expected.

Stopping for a rest, he noticed the hunched-back figure approaching the church from the south. As the man came closer, Tuck recognised him as Elias, an older man who lived alone, down by the banks of the River Calder. This was the first time the friar had seen him in, well, months now that he thought about it.

Elias had a very distinct gait thanks to his bent back, and it took him a while to reach the church. Every so often he would call irritably on the little brown dog that accompanied him. He didn't notice Tuck at the rear of the building as he shambled past, but there was such a look of anguish on his seamed face that the friar couldn't help but wonder what was wrong, and his curiosity was piqued even more when the aged man came into the church grounds.

"He's here to confess some sin," Tuck muttered to himself, returning to the stubborn door frame, another section of which broke into damp slinters as he struck it with his wooden mallet, sending half a dozen woodlice scattering into the shadows. He wondered what kind of wickedness the stooped old fellow could possibly get up to, alone by the river, and then wished the thought hadn't crossed his mind, for long years of experience told him that men could always find ways to do evil.

At last, all the rotten wood gave way beneath his blows and he was able to measure and cut the fresh, new sections. From there it didn't take too much time before he'd hammered it into place, chiselled out the hole for the lock, and nailed the door back into place. It wasn't the greatest piece of carpentry that anyone had ever completed, as the door fit rather too snugly, but he hoped it would all settle into place when the damp weather abated.

He stood back and smiled at his handiwork, quite proud of himself for he'd never fitted a door to a stone building before. Just then, Elias reappeared and, from his gloomy demeanour, Father Myrc had not been able to salve his conscience or offer much spiritual reassurance. Elias still bore an expression of great anguish, but that wasn't all, there was anger in his eyes too and, as he shuffled back towards his house in the south, all the while berating his little dog, Tuck decided it was time he went for some well-earned refreshments.

He headed around the side of the main church building to where Father Myrc's neat, low house was located. Knocking on the door and receiving a muffled response, he went inside, smiling at the priest who half-heartedly returned the greeting.

"Your storeroom door is fixed," Tuck reported. "Good as new." He wiped his brow exaggeratedly, eyeing Father Myrc as he did so and the priest, with a little snort of laughter, stood up, taking his meaning. He knew the friar well enough by now to understand his none-too-subtle requests for refreshment.

He came back carrying some bread, cheese, and a smaller cup of ale than Tuck would have liked. The priest merely smiled at his exaggerated, crestfallen look as he lifted the drink and took a dainty sip.

"Is the lock sturdy enough?" Father Myrc asked, watching as his friend bit into the cheese. "Can we get the tools back in?"

"Aye. No need to worry about thieves anymore," Tuck replied confidently. "You can check for yourself. Even Little John couldn't break that door down without an axe."

"Thank you," Father Myrc said, nodding in gratitude, but his face still seemed uncharacteristically grim to the friar and, without being prompted, he said, "You probably noticed old Elias visiting me. Yes, I thought you would." He sighed heavily, as if wrestling with his conscience. "He came to confess and, obviously, I should keep his words in confidence but…You are a man of God, so I suppose there's no harm in telling you what was said, and I could do with some advice."

Tuck put down his food and the ale cup and sat upright. His usual jocularity was gone, replaced by the deadly seriousness that showed his respect for matters of faith. He may have been an outlaw in the past, but his dedication to God had never wavered, and everyone in Wakefield knew it.

"You know that strange new sect that took over St Joseph's up in—" The priest broke off, shaking his head. "Of course you do, we've spoken about them before. The Disciples of God; John Little had a run in with them. Well, you know Elias married the lady who's in charge up there?"

Tuck stared at him, absolutely amazed at the revelation. "Elias married the Lady Alice? Are you jesting, old friend? She buried her husband, Henry, not six months ago!"

"Yes, I know that, but Elias…He's a lonely old fellow, stuck out there by the river, away from the rest of the village."

"That's his choice," Tuck noted.

"One he made when he was younger and had a wife and a family to keep him occupied. They all passed on over the years though and, when the Disciples of God came to the area, he was impressed by their holiness, and their teachings."

Tuck lifted his bread again and bit a section off, chewing slowly, as he cast his mind back to the gathering at St Joseph's the previous yuletide. Now that he thought of it, Elias had been there, and Tuck wondered now how he'd made it, given the distance, and the elderly man's stilted gait.

"As you probably know," Father Myrc continued, "Elias is quite, well…outspoken. He doesn't suffer fools gladly."

Tuck smiled. "Aye, I've seen him cursing youngsters in the village when he's come to market. Not a man to cross, even if he is getting on in years now."

"Agreed. Well, at first Elias was quite smitten by the Lady Alice – indeed I believe he still is although his bluff demeanour is rather hard to penetrate at times – and he accepted their practice of battling these so-called 'Black Lords'. I think he even joined in with them once or twice, waving his hatchet in the air against their invisible presence."

Tuck thought about that and didn't know whether to laugh or cry at the thought of stooped old Elias swinging his small axe around St Joseph's, accompanied by the rest of the Disciples of God with their swords and sharpened wooden stakes. It seemed absurd to the friar and, from the look on his face, Father Myrc too, but if that's how the Disciples chose to do God's work, that was up to them.

Besides, who knew?, Maybe there were Black Lords in the room with Tuck and the priest right at that moment, watching patiently, malevolently, waiting for a chance to work their evil.

Tuck shivered. No, the Disciples of God were not a matter for humour, the deaths of two men attested to that.

"So why was he here? If he's accepted the Lady Alice as his wife and spiritual leader, I mean."

"That's the problem," Father Myrc said. "He's grown disillusioned with them. He says he feels like a fool fighting invisible demons and doesn't believe what they say any more. In short, he's made a mistake in marrying the woman and wants away from her."

Tuck nodded. "That's unfortunate. It's always sad when a marriage is unhappy. I assume you told him he'd just have to get on with it."

The priest shrugged. "Of course, but you know Elias. He was not happy with that answer and pressed me for a way out of the marriage."

"I suppose he could get out of it if the Lady was a criminal," Tuck mused, gazing into his ale cup. "Little John certainly has his suspicions about the Disciples of God but, unless someone can prove any wrongdoing, Elias is stuck with his new wife."

"I did see one other possible solution," Father Myrc replied, and a wicked smile tugged at the corner of his mouth. "If he was impotent, and could not satisfy his wife's needs…"

Tuck laughed. "You old devil! I believe you're actually enjoying this."

Father Myrc looked sheepish then, and shook his head vigorously. "Not exactly, but…You must admit he *is* a cranky old fellow. He's forever falling asleep or muttering during my sermons; it's been the same for years. I must confess, I did take some pleasure in suggesting he claim impotence. Do you know what he said?"

Tuck imagined Elias would vehemently refuse such a course of action, but he was wrong.

"He told me," Father Myrc said, "rather angrily, that he really *was* impotent, and didn't give a damn who knew. But we'd have a hard time getting Lady Alice to agree to their marriage being annulled on those grounds, since the Disciples of God had all made vows of chastity anyway."

"Ah," Tuck replied. "That leaves him in a poor position then." He shrugged. "Why doesn't he just return to his home and ignore Lady Alice and her community at St Joseph's then? She's not likely to drag him back and force him to live with them."

"That," Father Myrc said, "is exactly what he's decided to do."

Now Tuck realised that was why Elias had come to Wakefield from the south, of course, rather than along the eastern road. "Far be it from me," he said, "to applaud a man for not honouring his marriage vows, but…I don't blame him. The Lady Alice seems very pleasant and holy, and the Disciples of God are apparently earnest in their beliefs, but there's something not quite right about it all."

"Oh, I completely agree," Father Myrc muttered, standing up and heading across to a table against the wall where he filled a cup with some communion wine for himself. "I don't trust sects like this. They often prey on the weak and could even be heretical; assuming they do hold any real beliefs at all, other than finding ways to fill their coffers with silver taken from the likes of Elias."

Tuck raised his cup in the air as Father Myrc raised his. "We agree on all of that, but until someone finds some proof, nothing can, or will, be done. Is Elias just going to forget all about them?"

"I suspect so," the priest replied, coming back across to retake his seat. "Although I have a feeling his wife will demand he supports her financially. But Elias is as stubborn as they come – I can see him taking any wealth he has and tossing it into the Calder, just to make sure the Disciples of God don't get their hands on it."

"You know," Tuck said thoughtfully. "Elias used to own the mill, just a little way upriver from his house. He sold it a few years ago, along with the land and, I believe, made a fair bit of money from the deal…"

Father Myrc sighed. "Of course. That explains a great deal about this strange union." He looked up at Tuck. "You've met the woman. What d'you think she'll do? Will she let Elias be? Agree to annulling their union, and move on?"

The friar thought about it for a long time, trying to draw a firm conclusion given their limited knowledge of the woman, and her sect, and of this particular situation with Elias until, eventually, he shook his tonsured head. "I have no idea. I actually wonder if we're doing Lady Alice a terrible disservice with all this talk. On the occasion I met her, she seemed a genuine, thoroughly likeable woman who feels she has a gift to share with the world. I didn't detect any duplicity in her and, generally, I'm a good judge of a person's character." He shrugged and stood up. "Time will tell. For the moment, we can do nothing and, since I'm done repairing your door, I'll make my way home and start dinner. God give you good day, old friend."

He didn't have far to go, but he walked slowly when Father Myrc waved him farewell, trying to remember Lady Alice; to come to some firm conclusion about her motives. He was none the wiser by the time he reached his house though and, when he closed the door behind him and sat down on his sleeping pallet, his exertions and Father Myrc's ale, caught up with him and he fell fast asleep, dinner forgotten.

CHAPTER TEN

It was pitch black when Tuck came awake, but years of living as an outlaw had honed his senses and he knew something wasn't quite right. He drew out the short cudgel he always had about him and more silently than most men of his girth, stood up, eyes fixed on his front door the whole time. He inwardly cursed when he realised he'd fallen asleep without even throwing the bolt across, but then there came a loud knock and an anxious call from outside and he hurried to open up, fears forgotten.

"Father Myrc," he said, peering out into the night at the priest. "What are you doing here at this hour?" He looked up at the moon's position and guessed it to be an hour or so past midnight. And then he realised the priest wasn't alone – a small, brown dog was wandering about at his back.

Elias's dog.

"What's happened?" Tuck demanded, going back indoors and lifting his quarterstaff as the priest replied in a voice filled with tension.

"I don't know. I got up to relieve myself and heard something moving about the church grounds. When I opened the shutters, there was the dog, just wandering about." He clasped his hands as if in prayer. "Of course, I recognised it straight away. It had been at the church just a few hours ago after all. You know who it belongs to, I assume?"

Tuck nodded. "There's no sign of Elias?"

"None that I can see. I did take a look around but…I will admit, Tuck, to being a little fearful, so I thought perhaps you could help? You know how to deal with things like this much better than I do."

There was no doubt in the friar's mind what his course of action should be. "Look," he said, grasping the priest's arm in a grip that was meant to soothe the churchman's nerves. "You can either wait here, in my house, with the dog, or take it home to the church. There should be no danger – the daft beast probably just escaped and came back to the village because it smelled a bitch in heat when it was here earlier." He smiled. "Let's be honest, Elias never ceases shouting at the poor animal. Would you not try and sneak off for some fun if you had the chance?"

Father Myrc raised his eyebrows as if he'd not thought of that solution to the dog's sudden appearance, and then he returned Tuck's small smile. "You're right, of course. I'll go home and take the dog with me. But what are you going to do?"

Tuck gripped his quarterstaff and his face became grim again as he replied, "To fetch Little John and Will."

* * *

"You really think a bunch of religious zealots have gone to old Elias's house and done him harm?" Will Scarlet appeared unconvinced, and unfazed by Tuck's suggestion. The friar had come to his house along with John and, although it was the middle of the night and his wife, Elspeth, hadn't been pleased at the disturbance, Will couldn't refuse his friends. Now, after a journey of almost two miles the three men were approaching their destination.

"I can see that bastard Colwin giving an old man a good kicking," John rumbled disdainfully. "Hopefully we can get there in time to repay him with similar treatment."

"Just be careful," Tuck murmured as they crouched now amongst the long grass that grew along the riverside. "Colwin and David are young men. Younger than us. Don't underestimate them."

"We've fought younger men before," Will replied as they finally saw the dark, squat shape of Elias's house in the light of the moon. "And always come out on top."

"Aye," Tuck admitted. "But not always unscathed. Just be careful – we've no idea what's happening here."

"Probably nothing," John said, and there was a hint of disappointment in his voice. "But we're almost there so we'd better be silent."

The three fell easily back into their old ways, with John taking the lead and the others following. As they came closer to the house they could hear voices and John turned to make sure Tuck and Will were aware that Elias was not alone.

The old man's house was a single-storey, low affair that looked as though it had been dumped on the ground rather than built piece by piece by skilled craftsmen. Despite that, the wooden structure had stood for decades and showed no signs of falling down anytime soon, attesting to the quality of younger-Elias's workmanship, if not his flair for architecture. The crescent moon was not bright enough to reveal the presence of anyone lurking outside the building so John led the way cautiously until they stood close to the front door.

It was shut, but through the open shutters on the nearest window a dim, flickering light told them at least one candle was burning within the house, and loud, male voices attested to the presence of more than one occupant. Elias had visitors, but how many it was impossible to tell.

John looked at Will and made a circling motion with his hand. Scarlet nodded and, wraithlike, disappeared around to the rear of the building as the giant bailiff and Friar Tuck strode up to Elias's door. Drawing deep breaths to steady themselves, John reached out with the end of his staff, preparing to rap it against the door.

Before he did so, the voices within grew suddenly louder but all they could hear was Elias, cursing his visitors and demanding they leave. His voice cut off mid-sentence, a sickening thud being the obvious reason.

"Burn the place down," came another man's voice, but John had already put all his considerable weight behind a kick that sent the door inwards, shattered off its very hinges.

The bailiff charged inside with Tuck at his back and, before the men inside could react, John had smashed his staff off the side of one of their faces, dropping the victim to the floor, dead or senseless but out of the fight either way.

The candle had been extinguished at some point in the past few moments and the room was almost completely dark now, but Tuck fended off one shadow with his own staff, while noting Will coming in through a rear window and struggling with another of Elias's tormentors. That fight didn't last long, ending in a cry of agony that Tuck hoped did not belong to his friend.

"Die, Black Lord!"

The shout came from directly behind Tuck and he instinctively swayed to the side, but not quite fast enough and it was his turn to cry out in pain as he felt something cut through his cassock and into his side. He was already turning though, spinning his staff which struck the weapon that had injured him, sending it flying against the wall with a metallic clatter. There was a cry of frustration as the attacker realised the fight was lost, and disappeared out through the smashed door and into the night. Strangely, the light scent of rose-water hung in the air in the wake of his departure.

"Are you all right, Tuck? Will?" Little John's deep voice broke the breathless silence and Tuck grunted a reply, sighing in relief when he heard Scarlet confirming he too was alive.

"They ran off into the trees, but we should check there's no more of them around," Will said, coming to stand at the front door beside Tuck. It was a little lighter there thanks to the moonlight coming through the entrance and he looked at the friar, noticing the drawn, unhappy features straight away. "Are you injured?"

Tuck nodded. "Aye, one of them slashed my side but I'm fine. We can dress the wound when we've made sure the area's clear."

John was beside them by now and, again, he led the way while the others brought up the rear. They stayed together, walking all the way around the house but finding no-one. When they headed back inside John took out his flint and steel while Will retrieved the candle and, between them, they brought it back to life. Its pale, yellow flame was welcome, but what it revealed was not.

"Bastards killed him," Will said, outraged at the violence visited upon Elias within his own home.

"Looks like a single blow to the head," John confirmed, leaning down and inspecting the dead man's cracked skull. "God's blood! If we'd been just a few moments earlier, we might have saved him."

Tuck had pulled off his cassock and was trying without much success to look at the bleeding wound just above his hip.

Will noticed his discomfort and came across to help. "Is it painful?" he asked, and Tuck nodded.

"Of course it bloody is. Have you not been cut by a blade before? Do I need to tell you what it feels like?"

"Look at this," Will said, bending to lift a dagger from the floor. "Must be what they cut you with."

"Let me see that," John demanded, reaching out to take it from his friend and eyeing the weapon with interest. "I recognise this," he said to the friar. "Don't you? This is the fancy knife Lady Alice held when she was talking about fighting Black Lords at the Christmas celebration, remember? One of her followers must have come here with it."

"That's ironic," Tuck growled. "One of the Disciples of God mistaking a friar for a demon." He grimaced as a sharp pain shot through his side. "Absurd. But never mind that. Will, can you find some wine around here so I can clean the wound? It's unlikely, but if the attackers come back, I'd rather not be sitting here half-naked."

"How many did we down? Two? Are they both dead?" John moved around the room as he spoke, checking the bodies on the floor. "That's a shame. We might have questioned them and come up with some evidence that the Disciples of God were behind this."

"Oh, I don't think there's any doubt about that," Tuck said, yelping as Will, who'd managed to procure a small jug of wine from Elias's pantry, poured the sour-smelling liquid onto his injured side.

"No doubt at all," John agreed. "But without evidence, there's not much we can do."

"We have these corpses," Will said angrily. "If we can prove they were members of that crazy sect, isn't that enough?"

"To prove the Lady Alice was behind the attack and see an end to her group?" Tuck replied. "No." He looked at John who was still walking about the house, trying to see if Elias's attackers had left anything behind that might incriminate them. "Do you recognise either of them? Brother Colwin or his quiet friend?"

John shook his head. "No. They're not here. I don't think I've seen either of those wasters before. No, wait – this lad." He stopped by the back window and took a closer look at the man Will had dispatched. "I have a feeling he's just a drunk from one of the nearby villages. If that's the case, the Disciples of God have simply hired some local scum to do their dirty work tonight."

Will found some old linen and, noting the fact that Elias no longer had any need for it, tore it into smaller strips which he used to tightly bandage Tuck's wound. It turned red with blood almost straight away, but Will assured the friar it was only a superficial cut and should give him no real trouble.

"Perhaps," the friar said, grunting as he drew his cassock back over his head and made it comfortable. "But the one who came for me shouted about the Black Lords, and the rest of the attackers must have escaped into the woods. I'd bet good silver that your friends, Brothers Colwin and David, were with them, if gambling wasn't forbidden by the Church."

"Well let's head to St Joseph's then," Scarlet said, fingering the pommel of his longsword. "You can arrest them there, John."

Tuck shook his head sadly. "There's no point, Will. Even if we found them, we can't prove they were here. The only real witness is dead."

"He's right," John admitted. "I've learned enough about the law in my time as a bailiff to know that, unless someone is already an outlaw, it takes a lot of evidence to prove them guilty. Especially someone wealthy and apparently respectable, like Lady Alice and her followers."

Will kicked one of the dead men on the floor angrily. "So, that's it then? We just go back to Wakefield and forget about what they did to him?" He nodded towards Elias.

"I don't know what we should do," Tuck said levelly, meeting Will's gaze and staring at the volatile ex-outlaw until he grew somewhat calmer. "We'll see what tomorrow brings. For now, however, I have no desire to walk all the way home. I say we toss the bodies outside, apart from Elias of course, and spend the remaining hours of darkness here."

All three of them were used to the proximity of death, having experienced it many times over the years; being an outlaw was a dangerous, often deadly, life after all. So, they helped one another haul the bodies outside, finding a handy tool shed nearby which was just big enough to store both of them. John smashed the lock with his quarterstaff and the dead men were unceremoniously heaped inside before the door was wedged shut with some large stones to make sure foxes or wolves didn't come and mangle them before they could be identified.

Then they went into the house, placed the smashed door back over the entrance as well as they could, and settled down to wait for sunrise. Tuck found more of Elias's wine in the pantry and handed it round to his companions but, even so, the following hours seemed to last forever and, at every noise they would start, and grasp their weapons while peering out the window in case the Disciples of God had come to finish what they'd started.

CHAPTER ELEVEN

"Well, I think it's obvious what we have to do," Patrick Prudhomme, Wakefield's headman, said the next day when John, Tuck and Will went to see him with news of Elias's horrible demise. "We call out the tithing and arrest every one of these Disciples of God. The sheriff and coroner can deal with them after that." He shook his head sorrowfully. "Elias wasn't much liked around here, but murder's a serious crime."

Tuck rubbed the night's growth of stubble on his usually clean-shaven chin and frowned at Patrick. "So, we arrest them, but without proof of their involvement they'll all go free and carry on as normal. Probably doing the same thing to some other lonely man, or woman, in one of the other villages around here."

Will touched his sword, as if he wished he could use it to exact revenge on those who'd taken Elias's life. He was a straightforward man, and spoke up now in a manner unsurprising to John and Tuck who both knew him well. "Why bother with the sheriff? We all bloody know what's happened, and why. If we turn up at St Joseph's, chances are they won't just let us arrest them. Then justice can take its natural course. With this." He patted his sword again, drawing an alarmed look from Patrick, and a nod from Little John.

"We can't just slaughter them all, by God," Tuck argued. "We have no idea how many of the group are involved. We're just guessing that Brother Colwin, with or without the knowledge of Lady Alice, is pulling the strings of the sect members. But, for all we know, neither of them had any part in last night's events. There could be some rogue element amongst the group. We'd not be doing God's work if we just arrived at the church and started killing everyone. As far as I can tell, at least some of them are genuine in their beliefs."

"Aye," John muttered. "But what exactly *are* those beliefs?"

"Do as their superiors tell them, even if it means murder," Will said, turning back to Tuck. "You're a true man of God. You've lived amongst devout, holy men within Lewes Priory, and I've done the same in Selby Abbey. Comparing those fools in the Disciples of God to the men we know is an affront."

Tuck smiled humourlessly. "Are you forgetting all the bad things Prior de Monte Martini did, Will? And what about those monks in Selby Abbey who almost killed your friend when you were living there?" He sighed. "Don't be so quick to judgement. We need to gather proof before we can seek justice for Elias's death."

"And Henry of Castellford," John put in. "And Brother Morris."

Patrick Prudhomme sat down heavily and stroked the head of the rangy dog that he'd taken in a year earlier. "Are you saying we do nothing, Tuck?" he asked in disbelief. "We don't even go and question Lady Alice and her followers about this? Look at your torn cassock – they could have seriously injured you!"

"No, we must do something," the friar said emphatically. "I would suggest John, as a representative of the king, carry word to the lady of her husband's vicious murder."

"Like she doesn't already know about it," Will sneered.

Tuck ignored him. "The coroner must also be summoned to carry out his duties and then," he looked at Will. "I think we must get someone inside the sect. To become one of them. That way we can truly get an idea of what they're up to."

There was silence within the small room as the men pondered Tuck's suggestion, and then Will laughed incredulously.

"Me? Are you saying I should join 'em? Have you lost your senses, Tuck?"

Patrick looked almost as uncertain as Will, but Little John eyed his volatile friend thoughtfully.

"It could work," the bailiff said. "You didn't come with us at Christmastime when we all went to their celebration. And later on, that night when David and Colwin came into the alehouse here, you had your back to them most of the time."

Tuck nodded. "Our table was in the shadows too."

"They'd recognise one of us, but they'll never recognise you," John finished.

"Don't look at me," Patrick said, raising his hands as if he wanted no part in this mad scheme. "I believe this kind of thing is what you men did when you were outlaws. God knows, there's enough stories told about you all. But I want no part of it. I don't want the sheriff blaming me when everything goes wrong, and St Joseph's ends up a bloodbath."

"Oh, ye of little faith," Tuck said with a glint in his eye. "You underestimate Will. He can keep his violent nature in check when he has to."

"Maybe," Scarlet retorted. "But it's not *my* violent tendencies I'm worried about!"

PART THREE – SUMMER 1330

CHAPTER TWELVE

As Tuck had expected, the coroner came to investigate Elias's death and some effort was put into identifying the two dead attackers who'd been stowed in the old man's tool shed. It wasn't an easy task, for it meant transporting the corpses, which were starting to decompose in the heat, around the nearby villages in a cart. Not a pleasant task for anyone. Both John and the coroner were heartily sick of the job by the time they'd visited just a couple of places without any success and, in the end, the bodies had to be buried before a single one was recognised. A lengthy description of each was recorded, just in case a relative reported them missing and they might be identified then from the coroner's records, but, in essence, the investigation went nowhere and the coroner was forced to give up without concluding who'd been responsible for Elias's murder.

He did talk with Lady Alice de Staynton but her shock and grief at losing another husband in a violent manner struck the official as genuine and she could provide no suspect or possible motive for Elias's murder.

Of course, John and Tuck had given their testimony, but they'd omitted any mention of the Disciples of God, fearing the coroner would frighten Lady Alice's group enough that they'd move on and simply begin afresh in a new county. Neither bailiff nor friar were willing to let that happen without Will Scaflock at least attempting to infiltrate the strange sect during the summer.

As it turned out, it was a simple matter to join the Disciples of God, for they were continually looking to add to their numbers. When Will turned up at St Joseph's three weeks later and asked to know more, Lady Alice, beaming a cheery welcome, brought him in and showed him around the old church. He could see why people liked her for she was charismatic and made him feel like he would be a valuable addition to their group.

There were some suspicious looks from a few of the male acolytes who saw Will and couldn't help but notice his muscular frame and soldierly bearing. It was perhaps understandable that such a man would be viewed with distrust, at least until more was known about his character. Will had no fears they would accept him soon enough for, although his short temper was so well-known that it had given him the nickname 'Scarlet', he was generally a good companion who could be as engaging and amusing as anyone in a conversation. His biggest fear was that he would be recognised, but it was a few years since he'd wandered Yorkshire and Nottingham as part of Robin Hood's infamous gang and, thus far, no-one had argued when he told them his name was William of Clipston and claimed to be nothing more than a former mercenary who'd taken a labouring job in a nearby village and wanted to do God's work.

He made a particular effort to smile warmly at Brother Colwin who was easy to spot from the description John had given him. The shaven-headed young acolyte did not smile in return, although he did nod, which was better than nothing and, after a few days, even managed a gruff, "God give you good day," when Will arrived for work in the morning.

John and Tuck had wanted Will to join the Disciples of God on the basis that he would actually live with them at the church, but he'd refused; he had a wife and a child to take care of after all. So, when Lady Alice accepted him into the group he started coming most days to help out around the place: tidying, tending the vegetable garden they'd planted, praying – which was quite catholic in nature, with no strange invocations or blasphemies – and, of course, battling the Black Lords.

Will had been allowed to simply watch the group the first few times they carried out this ritual, sitting on the floor of the church and staring in consternation at the sight of grown men and women hacking and slashing at thin air. A few even made angry sounds and curses during the 'fight'. It was clear to Will that some, if not all, of the acolytes genuinely believed they were in a battle for good versus evil, although their combat skills were sorely lacking. If the Disciples of God were literally defeating some malevolent entities in a real battle, Will concluded the Black Lords weren't up to much as fighters.

Colwin and David were a different proposition from the other Disciples of God, however. They knew how to wield a sword, moving with a speed and economy of movement that was impressive and necessary within the confines of the church with so many other, untrained, 'soldiers' flailing about beside them. It was obvious Will would have to be very careful around that pair.

Both those young men appeared totally devoted to Lady Alice, but then, so did all the acolytes. The holy woman seemed to have some personality trait which drew people to her, inspiring loyalty and even love. Young and old, men and women, all hung on her every word and gazed upon her with a reverence approaching, well, worship Scarlet thought.

Before he came to them, he expected Lady Alice to be physically attractive. To have some obvious allure that drew the likes of Colwin to her service – but she really was as plain as John had told him. She wasn't exactly a withered old hag, but neither was she the buxom, alluring woman he'd have thought young men would be drawn to.

"Are you all right, Brother William?"

Scarlet came to with a start. He'd been watching the acolytes battling Black Lords for a while and their uncoordinated movements, while amusing at first, soon became almost hypnotic and he'd fallen into a near-trance.

"What?" He looked up and forced himself to come alert, fearful he might say something to make his new fellows suspicious of his presence among them. "Oh, aye. Sorry, I think, er, I think I was being drawn into the battle against the Black Lords," he muttered, trying to hide the fact he'd almost fallen asleep with sheer boredom. "Time seemed to stand still for me."

Lady Alice put her back against the wall and slid down to sit on the floor beside him, an un-ladylike movement that seemed strangely endearing.

"Why aren't you leading them today?" Will asked her, knowing she usually directed the battle from the front, a task Colwin was doing this morning.

"It's good for them to learn from others," Lady Alice replied. "What if something happened to me? They need to be ready to continue, should one of us fall. Even me."

Will looked at her curiously. Was she suggesting there was something wrong with her? Did she expect to die? She was watching her acolytes battle invisible demons with a beatific smile on her face though, and appeared as healthy as anyone he'd ever seen, and he wondered if this was one of the ways she inspired people to follow her: to seem vulnerable, in need of their support.

She met his eyes and held out a hand to him as she pushed herself up. Flustered, knowing he couldn't refuse without seeming rude and perhaps opening an irreparable rift between them, Will took her outstretched hand and allowed her to help him rise.

"Come, Brother William," she said pleasantly. "You were a mercenary – you should be using your talents along with the rest of us, to defeat the Black Lords."

Still holding his hand, she led him to the very front of the group, being careful to avoid the wilder swings of the acolytes. Colwin watched them approach through narrowed eyes, and Will could tell the young man did not like this show of affection Lady Alice was bestowing upon the newcomer. Either oblivious, uncaring, or perhaps purposely goading Colwin, the Lady stopped directly in front of the shaven-headed acolyte and patted Will's sword.

"You know how to use that to battle human enemies," she said, nodding encouragingly. "Now, Colwin will direct you in the fight against the Black

Lords. Draw your weapon, Brother William, and prepare to meet the greatest threat the Christian world has ever known."

As she spoke, her face took on an intense, almost ferocious expression and she nodded vigorously at Will's sword until he slowly drew it out. The sunlight streaming through the windows reflected off the perfectly maintained steel blade and, again, Will saw Brother Colwin staring at him. The man radiated mistrust and barely controlled aggression and, without meaning to, Will found himself smiling.

He was not intending to goad the younger man; in fact, Will thought Colwin was very much like himself twenty years ago. Unfortunately, the tall acolyte misinterpreted Will's smile and his lip curled in distaste.

He thinks I'm mocking him, Will groaned inwardly. *As if this wasn't hard enough already, now this young fool will want to show me who's in charge here.*

And then he had to step sideways, as a woman swung a sharp stick around in response to Colwin's direction.

"Follow him, William," Lady Alice urged, copying Colwin herself although she had no weapon, just an empty fist. She, and the rest of the obviously unskilled Disciples of God, looked ridiculous, but the scene was too surreal to make Will laugh. He looked again to the shaven-headed young man at the front of the group, raised his sword, and began to follow along although with considerably more grace and finesse than any of the others.

At first, he felt self-conscious and utterly foolish, but then he decided to view it as a simple practice exercise and allowed himself to relax into a rhythm as he mimicked Colwin's moves, which started slowly and then became more vigorous. As the thrusts and swings became ever faster, Brother Colwin called out encouragement.

"There's one of the devils!" "Take his head off!" "Now, parry! Thrust, into its belly! Well done." "That's it, swing your weapon in an arc, keep them at bay. Look out!"

By the end of it, Will was sweating and actually felt more alive than he'd done since the fight at old Elias's riverside home. He looked around at the smiling Disciples of God who were congratulating themselves and each other on a successful battle with the terrible Black Lords, and he found himself grinning along and complimenting those nearest him.

It was utterly bizarre and yet, there was something thoroughly enjoyable and inclusive in it all. Will felt like he really belonged here with these kindly people.

"You were incredible!"

Will felt someone grasping him by the arm and he looked down at a wide-eyed, pale-faced woman of about thirty years.

"I can tell you know how to use your sword much better than any of us, other than Brothers Colwin and David," she gushed, still holding his arm tightly and gazing into his eyes. "You're going to be a great addition to our group. The Black Lords had better look out! Don't you think so, Denise?"

A young girl, perhaps twelve or thirteen, muttered something but refused to look up from the floor. She appeared embarrassed and Will guessed she'd rather be anywhere other than here in this old church. His heart went out to her for her shoulders were slumped and dejection radiated from her, but the older woman still had a hold of Will's arm and she gripped it tightly now to bring his attention back to her.

"Oh, don't mind my daughter. She misses her friends from home, but she'll settle here soon enough, just as we all have. Come on, it's time to prepare lunch, why don't you help us? William, isn't it?"

She pulled him towards the door for it was a nice day and the group were going to eat their meal outside in the summer sunshine – Lady Alice taught that fresh air and sunlight were essential for keeping the body healthy and in prime condition to defeat the unseen enemies that hovered around them every moment of the day.

As they passed Colwin he gave Will a cold look, although, surprisingly, he also nodded, as if in recognition of Scarlet's martial prowess. One warrior silently complimenting another. But then they were past and out through the tall doors into the church grounds along with the other acolytes moving around, gathering bread and meat and cheese and more things for what was to be a very pleasant lunch.

Simple tables had been set up and were soon laden with the food and drink as the Disciples of God talked to one another, happily discussing their morning's battle. Will noticed the young girl, Denise, seemed more comfortable out here, in a more natural, everyday environment. She was the youngest member of the sect, it seemed, and Will pondered that as Margaret found a seat for them at one of the tables. Was it right that a child should be forced to live among religious zealots? It wasn't his place to say, and the girl would have a nicer life than many other children in England, like the peasants who were forced to work from dawn until dusk every day to earn their keep.

If it had been his daughter, though, he'd have wanted her to grow up in a normal village, with normal people, and normal friends.

"How have you enjoyed your first few days amongst us, Brother?"

Will looked up at the question, which had been asked by a small man with a withered arm. Everyone at the table watched to see how he'd reply, and he smiled widely.

"I'm very happy to be here with you," he said, tearing off a piece of bread from the trencher Margaret slid towards him. "I hope I can do God's work alongside you all for a long time."

Everyone nodded and murmured agreement, thanking God and his saints for their good fortune and for Will's recruitment. When he bit into the bread and tasted how wonderful it was, then looked at the happy people surrounding him, he wondered why he was wasting his time there, deceiving them.

The Disciples of God were not murderers or heretics or anything else, as far as he could tell. They were good souls, most of them downtrodden, outsiders who'd found a home here with the Lady Alice, and it made Will feel guilty to be spying on them.

And then Brother Colwin, accompanied by Brother David, walked past, staring darkly at him, and he recalled Elias.

Perhaps most of the acolytes here at St Joseph's were innocent of any wrongdoing, Will thought, but those two were hiding secrets and he was perfectly placed now, as a welcome member of the Disciples of God, to find out what they were up to. Elias had not been a pleasant man even in his younger days, but he deserved justice and, when Will found proof that Colwin had been there at the old man's house the night he was murdered, that's exactly what would happen.

For now, however, it seemed to Will like the majority of the Disciples were nothing more than decent, God-fearing people.

CHAPTER THIRTEEN

"Will thinks he's wasting his time hanging around the Disciples of God," John said to Tuck two weeks after their friend had joined the religious group. "Spends too much time swinging his sword at thin air and listening to people blether on about God and the like. I'm not sure how much longer he'll stick it out, he's got work to do on his own farm."

Tuck smiled, and John did too. They both knew Will was no farmer – God above, even Will knew it. But he liked to do his best, and grew whatever crops he could, raised whatever livestock he was able. He was probably quite happy to get away from it all for a while, although a man like Will could only pretend to be something he was not for so long.

"And we've found nothing that would incriminate any of them," the friar said with a sigh. "Perhaps there's nothing *to* find."

John scratched his beard and watched the people of Wakefield go about their daily business. He'd met Tuck in the centre of the village and, although they were well-known and utterly conspicuous, no-one disturbed them. Their grim faces were enough to deter anyone with thoughts of small talk.

"There must be something we can do," the bailiff said in frustration. "Maybe we should just grab Colwin and drag him off. I'm sure Will could make him talk – Scarlet's good at stuff like that."

"We're not torturing anyone," Tuck replied with a firm downward stroke of his hand. "Not yet anyway.

Listen, remember that last little mystery we had, with the de Courcys, at Croftun Manor?"[2]

"Of course!"

"Well, I was thinking – one of the things that helped us figure that out was when I visited the records office in York to read the will."

John was nodding slowly as he began to understand where Tuck was going.

"We could pay the place another visit, and see if there's anything else we've missed, either in Henry of Castellford's or Brother Morris's wills."

"All right," John agreed, rolling up his sleeves for the sky was cloudless and it promised to be a hot day. "When do you want to go?"

"Now," Tuck said, rising to his feet. "We've no time to waste. If we can find something out before Will decides he's not going back to see the Disciples of God, maybe he can bring it up with some of the acolytes."

* * *

Will looked on as the Holy Mother brought the prayer session to an end, feeling quite bored by the whole thing. He liked a bit of a pray as much as the next man, giving thanks to God for his blessings and asking Him to take care of his loved ones who were in Heaven, but the Disciples of God took their 'prayers' to a ludicrous extreme. They would all gather, cross-legged on the floor of the church, and close their eyes as Lady Alice began talking in a soft, monotone voice that always made Will drowsy.

---

[2] See *Faces of Darkness*

She wouldn't even say very much, yet these sessions could last for over an hour and, by the end of them, Will would be stiff and thoroughly fed-up.

The other acolytes were a different matter, however. They would all fall into a trance, guided by the Holy Mother's instructions on how to breathe, so that Scarlet began to think some of them could quite easily never wake up again, and be quite happy with it.

These things simply didn't affect Will as they did the others though. He would sit in silence, bored and restless but knowing he couldn't excuse himself if he was to maintain the fantasy that he was a devoted member of the group.

Sometimes, as the cloying smell of incense suffused the air, one of the Disciples would start talking while in their trance, staring with sightless eyes at some invisible person or object in front of them. It could be a Black Lord or demon taunting them, or something more benign, like Christ himself or the Holy Grail. Today, Stephen Drinkwater had begun mumbling, little more than guttural noises in the back of his throat, as his eyes followed a mote of dust in the pale sunlight streaming through the stained-glass windows. His mutterings subsided after a time and all was silent until, at last, Lady Alice brought everyone back to reality with soft, calming words, and then gently rang a hand bell to signal the end of the ritual.

The Disciples, smiling—almost rapturous, Will thought—walked one by one to their Holy Mother, where they knelt and kissed her bare feet reverently. Some had tears streaming down their faces while others were laughing joyously and Will had to force a smile onto his own face as he too prostrated himself before the Lady and forced himself to lightly place his lips to her toes.

He was glad to get outside after that and wander about the grounds with the others, feeling the blood beginning to circulate in his stiff limbs once more. All this was not his thing at all, and he'd be glad when he could get back to his normal life in Wakefield.

"I get the impression you are not quite as invested in our prayer sessions as the rest of us, Brother William."

Scarlet turned and realised Lady Alice was walking next to him. He opened his mouth to deny the truth of her words, but she was smiling and he could tell any protestation would be swept aside. Instead he merely shrugged. "I'm just not as holy as the rest of you, I suppose," he said.

The Holy Mother put her arm inside his as they continued to walk, and she guided him away from the church. "There's no shame in that," she told him. "We are all created differently by the Lord and must work with the tools He saw fit to bestow on us. It says much for you that you continue to come to our group and work with us. God loves a trier, as the old saying goes."

"Maybe one day I'll see the light, like St Paul on the road to Damascus," Scarlet replied with a small smile of his own. "But, if not, I can at least help out around the church. I enjoy the hard work, at least." He wondered why she was bestowing her attention on him – she had no reason to think he was wealthy after all. Perhaps she saw him, with his expertly wielded sword, as a possible partner in crime for the next time she had to deal with a husband who, like Elias, proved to not be as pliable as expected.

She patted his arm and they walked on in silence for a little way, taking in the sight of the land that surrounded St Joseph's. Green grass and trees were broken here and there with little spots of colour, as blue and yellow wildflowers drew the eye, and purple dog roses grew against the outer wall of the church grounds, brightening the great stone beautifully in the sunshine.

The gentle sounds of insects busy about their work and the general feeling of a world at peace made Will relaxed enough to see what he could find out about Lady Alice's past.

Flattery, he decided, was the way to go.

"If you don't mind me asking, Holy Mother, how did you discover you were special?" He watched her as he spoke and, although she replied matter-of-factly, her lips twitched in a proud little smile.

"I was fourteen," she said, watching as a magpie sailed past, colourful plumage resplendent in the sunshine. "My mother died when I was only four years old, and my father was always distant. He was glad to see me married off to a wealthy magnate, despite the fact my husband was, at thirty, sixteen years my senior."

God above, how many times has she been married? Will wondered, but he kept his thoughts to himself as she went on.

"It was not a happy marriage. He would beat me regularly and...well, he would be unpleasant in other ways. I discovered that I could go into a trance at such times and the pain would be more bearable. Then, one day, I had a vision and I spoke with God."

Will was touched by her story and he listened intently as they walked on in a wide oval that would eventually bring them back to the front gates of St Joseph's.

"Anyway, I fell pregnant when I was fifteen and, when I lost the baby, I started to have more visions and more experiences of God and, frighteningly, the Black Lords. My husband found out and accused me of being a witch and, terrified that his social standing would suffer, he cast me out of our home and bribed a bishop to declare our marriage unlawful."

"Did you go back to your father?"

"I tried," she growled with barely restrained anger. "But he wanted nothing to do with me, not when he heard the lies my former husband told him. I was alone."

"What did you do?" Will asked, greatly intrigued.

"There was a holy man in the town where I grew up. Not a normal priest, or friar—he was full of life and energy and taught his followers about the true power each of us holds within us, if we can just find a way to harness it." She shrugged as if what followed next was completely natural, given her special powers. "When he died, the group saw me as his successor, even though I was still just sixteen years old. Ever since then I've been going from place to place, taking the battle to the Black Lords, helping my Disciples to find their way in the world, and doing good works."

They'd returned to the church by now and Lady Alice let go of Scarlet's arm. She had a sad, haunted look in her eyes as she gazed at him, and, strangely, he would have liked to reach out and hold her close, comfortingly. It struck him then that her whole story had been a performance, designed to instil exactly this kind of reaction, and he wondered how many people she'd told it to over the past twenty or thirty years, and how many of them had fallen deeper under her spell as a result. Was her tale even true? He couldn't tell.

None of this showed on his face though and they parted ways, she walking into St Joseph's, while he, desiring the warm sunshine on his face to take away the chill that had suddenly settled in his soul, went to sit with Sister Margaret and some of the other Disciples who were smiling and chatting happily together within the grounds.

* * *

The records Friar Tuck and Little John wanted to see were housed in the basement of a building within the grounds of the great cathedral in York. The last time Tuck had been there he'd had to persuade the clerk in charge, a small priest with an officious nature, to give him access to what he wanted, but he'd made a lasting impression on the man so this time there was no problem. Especially with Little John's menacing presence practically filling the small office.

With the clerk's help—he was fiercely proud of his filing system and knew where everything was within the gloomy, fusty smelling basement—Tuck was quickly able to locate what he was after. First, he read over Henry of Castellford's will, but found nothing new within it. Things were just as they'd been told, so the document was soon placed back exactly where the priest had taken it from.

"Now, Brother Morris's," the friar said, drawing a frown from the clerk.

"I'll need more than that," the man grumbled, gesturing at the rows of records filling the great, dark room. The pitiful light from their candles didn't even stretch to the back walls. "We could search all day and not find it. Narrow it down, man."

Tuck nodded. "Forgive me, of course...Well, he died within the boundary of Altofts; that's the closest village to St Joseph's."

"When?"

"Just before Christmas. St Lucy's Day."

"Perfect." The clerk allowed a small, rare smile to light up his face for a brief moment and he led them towards a cabinet further into the blackness. The candles slowly banished the gloom as they walked, casting eerie shadows all about them, but it only took moments for them to reach their destination.

The clerk ran his finger along the shelf and then drew out a scroll and carefully, almost reverently, unrolled it. "Morris de Vere," he said, peering at the name written on the top of the document. "Died by his own hand on the Ides of December, in the year of our Lord thirteen twenty-nine. This'll be your man, I think."

With a glad smile Tuck took the scroll to a desk nearby and sat down, placing his candle beside himself.

"That was impressive," Little John said, and for some reason his usual booming voice was soft, as if he feared to disturb the shadows, and the written accounts of births, deaths, marriages and so on that were housed within the dusty room. "Finding the will so fast, I mean."

The clerk looked at him suspiciously, wondering if he was being made fun of then, seeing the bailiff was deadly serious, made a dismissive noise. "Not particularly, big fellow. Only one person died in Altofts that week!" With that, he waved a hand and headed for the door and the steps leading back up to his office. "I've got work of my own to do. You two make sure the document's returned exactly where you saw me take it from, all right? And lock the door at your back."

He hurried away and, when he was safely out of range, John laughed softly. "You'd think he was guarding the king's own treasures the way he behaves."

If he expected Tuck to agree, he was disappointed for the friar was thoroughly engrossed by Brother Morris's last will and testament. His lips moved soundlessly as he read and he used his finger to mark his place as he read for, despite the candle next to him, it was quite dark in the room and Tuck's eyes weren't what they'd once been. It didn't take long for him to exhale loudly in excitement, and John came over to stand behind him, peering down over his shoulder.

"What is it?"

Tuck looked up, eyes shining in the candlelight. "There's a second page!"

John's brows drew together. "You mean one you didn't read the night the fellow died in St Joseph's?"

"Aye," the friar agreed. "Which makes me wonder…" He fell silent and began reading this second sheet of parchment, eyes moving rapidly along the Latin words, most of which were impenetrable to the big bailiff. Every so often he'd murmur but continued to ignore John's impatient questions until he finished scanning the document.

"Well? In God's name, Tuck, I can see you've found something interesting. Tell me!"

"Brother Morris had a terrible disease," the friar said grimly. "It was killing him."

John frowned. "You mean like Henry of Castellford?"

"Exactly like that," Tuck replied, running his finger along a line in the will. "A surgeon, whom he names Gilbert, diagnosed him on the third day before the Kalends of September, and his health had been growing worse since then." He met John's gaze. "Like Henry, he thought his suicide would not be counted as a sin, for he was sacrificing himself to battle the Black Lords in Purgatory."

"This is madness," John exploded. "There's no way it can be mere coincidence – someone fooled them into taking their own lives and leaving their wealth to the Disciples of God. And it's pretty damn obvious who." He trailed off but there was a murderous gleam in his eyes.

"This is still not enough though," Tuck muttered, eyeing Brother Morris's will as if some other, hidden, piece of incriminating information might be hidden there. "All it shows is a certain madness on the part of the two dead men. There's nothing to say anyone drove them to it."

John shook his head, clenching his fists in a gesture that Tuck knew from long experience. "This can't go on, old friend," he said firmly. "If we don't do something more men will die. I won't just stand by and let that happen. We have to at least accuse Lady Alice and Brother Colwin. Bring this out in the open so their other acolytes aren't blind to what they've been doing."

Tuck stood and rolled the parchment up, then he walked over and replaced it exactly where the clerk had drawn it from originally. "Perhaps you're right," he sighed. "I didn't want to tip them off to the fact we're wise to them though. Oh well, maybe by the time we get back to Wakefield, Scarlet will have discovered something else we can use against them."

John forced a smile as they took their candles and headed out of the basement, locking the door securely behind them. "Aye, maybe he'll have charmed Lady Alice into telling him everything."

Tuck laughed shortly. "Perhaps. But it's more likely he'll have beaten Brother Colwin half to death trying to force a confession from him! Come on, let's get home as quickly as possible."

CHAPTER FOURTEEN

"Defend yourself, old man!"

Will threw up his sword and knocked his attacker's blade aside, not particularly surprised by the ferocity of the blow. All summer, Brother Colwin had seemed to feel threatened by Will's presence within the Disciples of God and today, with a chill wind blowing around the churchyard, Lady Alice suggested the acolytes do some real sparring with one another as practise for the metaphysical battles with Black Lords.

Colwin immediately sought out Will. Although Scarlet thought it was a bad idea, he couldn't really back down from the fight.

Well, he could have backed down – indeed, if Tuck were there he would admonish Will for accepting the younger man's challenge – but he was not one to walk away from an arrogant fool looking to be taught a lesson.

The thought that he, himself, might be injured in such a bout never crossed Scarlet's mind.

Until now.

Brother Colwin battled invisible Black Lords convincingly, and even carried himself like a soldier, but Will had not really expected him to be such a challenge. Little John had apparently pinned him against the wall without much effort after all. But the shaven-headed acolyte was quite skilled with a sword and, as he lunged once more, Will was forced to dodge desperately to the side or be skewered.

Lady Alice looked on with interest but didn't upbraid Colwin for his viciousness, and Will wondered if she would be bothered if one of them died here.

Well, it wouldn't be him.

Smashing aside Brother Colwin's next attack, Will kicked out, aiming for his opponent's bollocks. He missed, but the heel of his boot dragged down Colwin's thigh, drawing a cry of pain. For the first time, the Disciple's face showed a spark of uncertainty as he stared at his opponent who, although in his forties now, retained the stocky build and heavily muscled arms that had served him well during his years as an outlaw.

"A cowardly move, Brother," Colwin growled, clenching his jaw in anger, but Lady Alice shook her head.

"You know the Black Lords do not fight fair, Colwin. William will give you a proper test, so the next time you face our enemies you'll be even better prepared."

"Aye," Will grinned, parrying another slash. "Men don't fight fair, Colwin. Why would Black Lords?"

"Do you mock us?" Colwin demanded, eyes blazing with righteous anger. "Do you think our mission a joke?"

Their swords connected and the pair stared into one another's eyes, evenly matched as they sought to force their opponent onto the back foot. Will was surprised at how strong the younger man was – Colwin didn't look that heavy but he seemed quite capable of holding his own in this test of strength. After a few moments Colwin's stamina began to flag however, and, seeing the discomfort on his face, Will gritted his teeth and pushed with all his might, breaking the deadlock and sending Colwin stumbling backwards. Taking advantage of his sparring partner's poor footing, Will rained blow after blow down on the hapless acolyte and then, changing tack, swept his leg around, tripping Colwin.

Scarlet smiled in triumph and spun his sword so he could aim the point at his downed opponent's chest and demand he yield. Much to his astonishment, Colwin, from a position flat on his back on the grass, somehow used his arms to lever himself back onto his feet in a blur of motion and, in an instant, his sword was slicing through the air towards Will's torso.

Crying out in surprise, Will just barely managed to throw his own blade up, knocking his attacker's weapon to the side, but it wasn't a clean block and the sharp steel cut through his sleeve, opening a long gash in his forearm. Breathlessly, the men stepped back as blood began to ooze from Will's injury.

"What's wrong, old man?" Colwin smiled coldly. "Frightened?"

On the contrary, it took a lot more than a bloody wound to frighten Will – this had just brought his legendary temper boiling to the surface. With a curl of his lip, he aimed a cut at Colwin's legs but, when the acolyte shifted to avoid the blow, Will dropped his sword and launched himself forward. Grabbing his opponent by the throat, he swept his legs away again, but this time, when Colwin collapsed onto his back, Will dropped on top of him, forcing his knees into Colwin's midriff.

Furiously, the shaven-headed Disciple tried to throw Will off, but Scarlet was too powerful, and too experienced in the ways of war, and he pressed tighter on Colwin's neck until the young acolyte's face began to turn a livid shade of purple.

"Stop! Brother William, please stop!"

It was Margaret, who looked shocked and sickened by the violence that had suddenly exploded in front of them all. Will stared at her, and then turned his head towards Lady Alice who was now flanked by Brother David. Those two looked on impassively, as if they cared not at all about Colwin's fate. Indeed, Alice seemed to be positively enjoying the entertainment, her eyes burning with an inner fire that instantly cooled Will's own hot anger.

He released the pressure on Colwin's throat and stood up, watching as the Disciple rolled onto his hands and knees, coughing and retching and struggling to catch a breath. Margaret ran to him, touching his shoulders and asking, rather redundantly, how he felt.

Will looked at his arm. It wasn't a deep cut, but it was bleeding quite heavily and beginning to ache a little.

"Brother David," said Lady Alice to her silent companion, both still watching Scarlet intently. "Fetch some strips of cloth, and water to clean Brother William's wound."

Instantly, the man hurried into St Joseph's as the lady smiled and waved her hand at the other Disciples who remained frozen, staring at Will and the downed Colwin. "Come on now," the Holy Mother called brightly. "Everything is all right. No serious injuries.

Let's see the rest of you put as much effort into your training as the two brothers here."

The others in the group looked uncertain, but Lady Alice's smile and calming presence soon had them back sparring, focused on their own tasks and the tense atmosphere returned to normal at last.

Will sat down at one of the tables they'd eaten lunch at and waited for Brother David to return with the medical supplies. He wasn't sure what to do next – he didn't really want Colwin as an enemy, so the idea of going across to check on the red-faced acolyte crossed his mind but, before he could move, Lady Alice joined him and the moment was gone.

"That was very impressive," she said. "Oh, here's the bandages. Roll your sleeve up, go on."

Will did as he was told, and the Holy Mother took the bowl of water and strips of cloth from David who she then dismissed with a nod. She bathed his injury, rinsing the blood down onto the grass below with the water, which Will noted smelled of rose-petals, and then she dried his arm with a strip of cloth and used another to bind the wound. When it began to turn red, she added a second strip and then rinsed off her hands with the rose water.

Colwin watched them with a murderous expression and Will found himself wondering just what in God's name was really going on within the Disciples of God, for Colwin's dark look was that of a spurned lover. Weren't these people supposed to have made a vow of chastity? Perhaps they had, and Colwin's feelings were akin to those of a love-struck youngster. If the acolyte had made his vow of chastity years before, there was a good chance he was still a virgin.

Will couldn't imagine what that would make a person feel like.

Even Tuck had been with women in his life, before he became a friar.

This whole mad scheme was getting too complicated, and Will knew he had to get out of it before it was too late. Three men had already died, and chances were high that either he or Colwin would be next.

He was glad he didn't have to sleep at St Joseph's every night.

Lady Alice was talking again, and he forced his attention back to her. "Perhaps," she was saying, "you should lead the fights against the Black Lords from now."

"Me?"

"Yes. You're clearly the best warrior in the group, so it makes sense that you should lead us. Don't you think?" She smiled again. She always seemed to be smiling. "I can see you're too modest to agree with me. Think about it. Oh, I know what you're thinking: Brother Colwin's nose would be put out of joint if you took his place. But he's completely loyal to me, and the group. He'll do what's best for us, don't worry."

She stood up, touching his injured arm softly and then went off, into the interior of the church where the wind that heralded the coming of autumn wouldn't bite so hard.

Colwin, Margaret, and everyone else in the group were looking at him, with various expressions on their faces. It struck Will that Lady Alice's behaviour could be seen, in other circumstances, as seductive. If he were in an alehouse with Little John, for example, and a couple of women had joined them and behaved as the Holy Mother did, Will would think they were looking for more than just a drink. The little touches, the smile, the dipped eyelashes. Perhaps this was connected in some way to three male Disciples meeting their end in recent weeks.

And yet, Will mused, Lady Alice was not that attractive. He personally had no interest in bedding her, even if her vows didn't preclude such a union, and he wasn't happily married. He looked at Margaret – she was younger, prettier, and had a vulnerability about her that Will found much more appealing than the Holy Mother's confidence and air of command. Yet the male acolytes didn't seem to view Margaret as anything other than a friend.

He was certainly starting to feel like the Disciples of God loved their Holy Mother in more than just a platonic fashion though. Somehow, that made him feel more sympathetic to them.

He got up and, acting completely out of character, walked over to Brother Colwin who grasped the hilt of his sword and narrowed his eyes at Scarlet's approach.

"Are you all right?" Will asked, forcing his voice to sound as friendly as possible, as if he were truly concerned for the young fool. "I'd no intention of really hurting you – you're a skilled fighter, caught me off guard and, well…" He grinned and nodded at the bloodstained bandage on his arm. "I lose my temper when I get injured."

Colwin glared at him in cold silence, but Margaret spoke up.

"You men are like children," she scolded. "We're all friends here. Brothers, you two are supposed to be! Your fight is with the Black Lords, not one another."

In reply, Colwin stood up, towering above the slight figure of the blonde woman and then, with a sneer at Will, turned and stalked away, disappearing into the church without a backward glance.

"Don't mind him," Margaret muttered, trying to smile. "He's a good man, who takes our holy work very seriously. He's just…A little bit lost, like all of us here. You've hurt his pride – he was supposed to be the strong warrior of the group. The protector. He probably thinks you're taking that away from him."

"He's wrong," Will said. "I've no interest in anything other than keeping my head down, praying to God, and battling the Black Lords with the rest of you." He shook his head irritably, unable to entirely hold his temper in check. "But he's lucky I didn't hurt him more. He was trying to maim or even kill me, and, normally when someone does that, they don't get up and walk away."

Margaret, in contrast to Lady Alice, looked singularly unimpressed by Scarlet's words.

"What's his story anyway?" Will asked her quietly. "Why is he here?"

She frowned. "I'd have thought that was obvious. He's here because he believes in our work: battling Black Lords and helping people in need."

"You all really believe in the Black Lords, do you?"

"Some more than others, perhaps," she admitted before her face softened and she went on. "I don't know the full story, but I do know that Colwin trained to be a soldier. For whatever reason, he decided his life would be better spent in God's service rather than the king's, so he joined us a year or two ago. He's devoted to the Holy Mother, and our work, and he'll do anything to defend us."

The woman clearly held great affection for Brother Colwin but Scarlet said, "He might have killed me today."

"Well, he didn't, and we Disciples of God believe in forgiveness, Brother William," she said, holding his gaze. "So, I hope you can forget what's happened today and move on from it. Now…Shall you be having your evening meal with us before you go home to your own village?"

Her haughty gaze faded, and her words were inviting, but Will wanted to get back to Wakefield as soon as possible, that he might talk with Tuck and John about everything that had happened, and his thoughts on the sect that he was, for now, part of. So, thanking her, he waved farewell to them all, mounted his old palfrey, and headed north to his supposed home village of Methley before turning southwest at last and riding hard for Wakefield.

CHAPTER FIFTEEN

"Thank you, Amber, this stuff is superb." Will took a sip of the freshly brewed ale Little John's wife had handed to him and practically purred like a cat.

Friar Tuck was also there for they had agreed it was too dangerous to continue meeting in the village alehouse, since the Disciples of God might turn up on another recruiting mission and see 'William of Clipston' drinking with the bailiff who'd been asking questions about old Elias's death. It would wreck their scheme completely, so Scarlet and the friar had come here, to Little John's house, where they could talk in private. Amber knew them well and was always happy to see one or both of them, for they were good company and good support for John who, especially in the early days, struggled at times with his role as a bailiff.

"I always said you were the best at brewing ale." Tuck nodded vigorously, placing his own mug down on the table and helping himself to a refill from the big jug Amber had provided. "Best in the whole village."

"Best in Yorkshire," John agreed, winking at his wife playfully. "And not just at making ale!"

"You better believe it," Amber laughed. "But don't be sitting there drinking all night, the three of you. I don't want you rolling home to Elspeth, Will, drunk and singing and waking little Blase from his sleep."

She threw on a cloak and bent to kiss John on the cheek. "I'll leave you to it. I'm going to visit Hilda – she's got some gossip about young Dickon, the farrier's apprentice. You'll have the house to yourselves for a bit, all right?"

She went out and they heard her humming cheerily to herself through the closed door until she was out of earshot. John had a son with her, also named John, but the lad was sixteen now and training to become a forester, which meant he spent many of his nights, like this one, away at the manor house.

They were alone, and could speak freely, and Tuck could tell Will had been bursting to tell them his news ever since he'd arrived at John's home.

"What's happened?" the friar demanded. "I see you're favouring your left arm instead of your right. Were you injured at St Joseph's?"

Will rolled up his sleeve, not surprised that his friend had already noticed he was wounded, despite the material of his new tunic covering it. With the help of his wife, Elspeth, he'd taken off Lady Alice's rather crude bandage and then properly cleaned and re-dressed the gash. It was still leaking a little blood, which both Tuck and John muttered at, but it would heal well enough in time.

"Don't tell me," the bailiff growled. "You got into a fight with Brother Colwin."

"How did you guess?" Will replied with a grim smile.

"You didn't kill him, did you?" Tuck groaned. "Maybe it wasn't such a good idea to ask you to join their group after all."

Will looked offended. "Don't be so quick to judge," he said, quoting the friar's own oft-repeated line. "I was attacked by Colwin – he did that to my arm when we were sparring. I just defended myself before he could do any more damage. I'll tell you though: he's devoted to that sect, and truly believes he's doing God's holy work. You can see it in his eyes."

"But did you *kill* him?" John asked, repeating Tuck's earlier question. "Please tell us you didn't let that temper of yours—"

"No, I didn't bloody kill him," Will cried. "I put him on his arse and almost strangled him, but he's all right. He'll think twice about attacking me like that in the future."

"Or he'll just be more sneaky about it," Tuck said. "You'll have to be even more vigilant around them. What happened anyway?"

Scarlet recounted the day's events, finishing with his belief that the male Disciples of God were probably all in love with Lady Alice, and that idea set both Tuck and John nodding in understanding.

"That makes sense," the friar said. "And it fits with what we discovered ourselves today in Pontefract." He proceeded to fill Scarlet in on the contents of Brother Morris's will, tying it in with Henry of Castellford's similar document bequeathing his estate to Lady Alice and the Disciples.

"It seems," John said, "that the Holy Mother uses her charisma to draw in wealthy men, and then somehow persuades them to take their own lives, leaving everything to her. Undoubtedly, old Elias would have suffered the same fate if he hadn't been such a cantankerous old sod, and seen through their blasphemous sect before Alice had a chance to make him write out his will."

"Not that it matters," Tuck noted. "They were legally wed before he was murdered. The Lady gets everything anyway, will or no, since he has no other surviving family."

"I'm starting to think the woman values money over any spiritual calling," Scarlet said. "There was a young man from Leeds at the church with us for a couple of days. He'd had a bad time of it from what I could gather, and needed help." Scarlet shook his head. "He wasn't there today. I asked Margaret about it and she said the Lady had sent the fellow home—not suitable for the Disciples of God apparently."

"Why?" Tuck asked curiously. "What was wrong with him."

"He was a peasant," Scarlet replied, and all three leaned back on their stools with knowing looks on their faces. "Oh, that's not the reason the Holy Mother gave, but it seems obvious – there's no poor folk amongst the Disciples. Everyone is well-spoken, well-educated, and well-off."

"They all have something material to offer the group," Tuck murmured darkly. "Especially when they die and leave it all behind for the Holy Mother."

The friends sat nursing their drinks, the ale's dark, fresh taste forgotten now as they contemplated the deaths of three men, drawn into the web of a woman who professed to be sworn to God but was, perhaps, every bit as wicked as the Black Lords her sect claimed to oppose.

"I don't get it," Will muttered, rubbing his stubbled chin in bafflement. "The woman does nothing for me. I can't understand why men are falling over themselves to be with her. They don't even lie together, these Disciples. They're all celibate!"

"So they say," John muttered darkly. "Who knows what they really get up to? They could all be at it right now in that old church—"

Tuck broke in before the bailiff could go into any details of what might be happening in St Joseph's at that moment. "To answer your question, Will, about why men are attracted to Lady Alice, even though you personally don't find her attractive." He leaned back on his stool and crossed his arms. "Think about it. You, my friend, are married to a woman much younger than yourself."

"Much, *much* better looking too," John said, laughing at the un-Christian oath Will spat at him in return, but Tuck went on, ignoring their banter.

"You have Elspeth, Will. You have a new son. You have your daughter, Beth, and your grandchild, Robert." Tuck continued, ticking things off on his fingers as Scarlet listened in silence. "You have your farm, you have wealth, you have two handsome friends."

"Who?" John demanded before taking Tuck's meaning and laughing sheepishly.

"You have everything a man could ask for, Will," the friar finished. "But think back to when I first met you in Barnsdale – an outlaw, a widower…" He trailed off, not wanting to remind his friend too much of those terribly dark times. "Imagine if you had met Lady Alice at that point, and she'd been friendly and caring and made you feel like you belonged. Would you have rejected her, or would you have felt something like Henry of Castellford or Brother Morris?"

Again, the three sat in pensive silence, the atmosphere turned maudlin by Tuck's reminiscences. His words made perfect sense, and offered an insight into how heretical sects – some benign, some setup purely for reasons of self-aggrandizement or accumulation of personal wealth – were able to grow, despite seeming crazy to most normal people.

"It makes sense, I suppose," Will said. "When you feel like you've nothing, and someone offers you *something*...Aye, I see your point."

"I'm sorry Will, I didn't mean to bring up the past again."

Scarlet had turned away from them for there were tears in his eyes which he did not want them to see, and John spoke up, drawing the attention back to himself.

"So, going forward, Will should look out for Lady Alice's next target, and then we can intervene before the lovestruck fool kills himself!"

Tuck smiled, shaking his head at John's bluntness. "Yes, and in the process get some proof that this is what the Lady is doing, so we can bring her to trial."

Will turned back to them, in control of himself once again. "I was hoping I wouldn't have to go back," he admitted. "They live a pretty boring life."

"Only you would think having your arm slashed open in a sword fight was boring," Tuck replied. "But I'm sorry, if you can stick it out a little longer, I'm sure we'll be able to stop the Holy Mother from causing another man's death."

"I'll drink to that," John said, refilling all their mugs and hoisting his aloft in salute. The others joined him in the toast, although the bailiff rather soured it by adding, "This is all assuming Lady Alice is the main instigator, and not Brother Colwin."

Tuck wiped ale from his upper lip and looked to Will. "Could it be Colwin pulling the strings?"

Scarlet was tempted to refute the suggestion immediately, for he'd seen the young acolyte watching Lady Alice like a besotted puppy, but he thought about it for a moment before responding.

"No, Colwin isn't the one making men fall in love with the Holy Mother, she's doing that herself, obviously. But," he held up a hand before John could comment. "Colwin is full of rage and he's clearly capable of violence." He nodded towards his slashed arm. "So it wouldn't surprise me to find out he was the one that led the attack on Elias. In fact, I'd say that's exactly what happened, for I can't see the Lady getting her hands dirty in a situation like that. She's the brains, and Colwin's the muscle."

"It's just a shame we didn't reach Elias's house a little earlier," John said in exasperation. "We might have caught Colwin and ended this whole thing already."

"True," Tuck said, a mischievous gleam in his eye. "But that's both of you he's injured now. If it comes to another fight with Colwin, you'd better let me deal with him."

"Shut up, Tuck," Will retorted with a good-natured laugh. "And drink up. It's time we were off to our own homes. Come on."

They emptied their mugs and got up to go, making small talk about one another's plans for the rest of the night, and family and so on, then John said, "Joking aside, Scarlet, you should be careful when you're with the Disciples. Even if most of the members are innocent of the crimes we're blaming Colwin and the Lady for, they'll not be slow in supporting them if they think you're not who you claim you are."

"Oh, I'm well aware of that," Will replied as he and Tuck headed out into a night that was about as warm as it would get now that autumn was around the corner. "I'll watch my back."

"Don't take any chances," the friar added. "We don't want you to be their next victim."

With that, John waved them goodnight and closed his door, settling back into his chair and contemplating this whole unpleasant business as his two friends wandered off to their own homes.

Not one of them noticed the tall figure crouching in the bushes to the rear of Little John's house. Not one suspected their every word had been overheard and, by the time Amber returned from her friend's house, bursting to share her gossip with John – who enjoyed prattling as much as his wife – the dark shape had hurried off, mounting a nearby horse and riding north-east.

Towards St Joseph's.

PART FOUR – AUTUMN/WINTER 1330

CHAPTER SIXTEEN

Scarlet didn't return to the church in Altofts for a few days, having work on his own farm he had to deal with before he could travel to St Joseph's again. When he got there, he noticed Brother Colwin kept his distance and, other than some dark, suspicious looks, did not bother him. This was much better than Will had expected, since he really didn't want to hurt the younger acolyte any more than he already had, so the day passed relatively easily.

Lady Alice spoke to him a couple of times but she seemed to realise Will was not the type of man who would fall in love with her as easily as the others and, as the week progressed, she came to him less and less. When she did seek him out it was merely to ask how he was, how he was finding the work – he was helping the other disciples to weave baskets for sale at the local markets during those days – and other trivial matters.

Without the scrutiny of Colwin and Alice it meant Will could chat more freely with the other members of the sect. As he carried sacks of material or lifted completed baskets onto wagons for transportation to market, he made small talk with mostly the male Disciples. He was careful with his conversation but always managed to find a way to ask about the person's financial situation via seemingly innocent chatter about their background, previous life before they joined Lady Alice's group, and what had made them come here to St Joseph's with the others.

Unsurprisingly, Will discovered that most of the men were far from poor, although a handful had lost a portion of their wealth through some trouble in their life, be that a problem with drink, or the law, or family. Many of the men were still landowners, however, and what most people would consider 'well off', although some seemed too sensible to be fooled by the scheme he believed Lady Alice was orchestrating around the more vulnerable acolytes.

One, however, fit the template closely. Stephen Drinkwater was in his fifties and had the hunched posture of a man beaten down by life's misfortunes. Unlike the other members of the sect, Stephen wore a pig-hair shirt, shaved his beard without water, and abstained from wine or rich foods, all in the belief these earthly hardships would bring him closer to God. He was, like most people, quite content – even eager – to talk about himself, telling Will about his childless marriage to a wonderful woman who'd died five years earlier, leaving a gaping hole in Stephen's heart which had never begun to heal until he joined the Disciples of God. His working years had been spent collecting taxes, a job which had worn him out, mentally, over the decades, as he saw poor families suffering every time he visited a town or village to carry out his job. In contrast to those malnourished men, women and children, Stephen had taken his wages and invested in a trading company run by one of the noblemen in his hometown. The investment had grown remarkably and, by the time he was fifty, he was a wealthy man, ready to enjoy a simple, comfortable life with his beloved wife.

And then she died, and he'd been utterly lost. Without children or any other surviving family, and never a popular man thanks to his hated profession, Stephen had entered a dark, lonely period of his life, one which he'd expected would end in an early grave at the bottom of a wineskin.

Lady Alice had come to his town with her group – half the size it was now – and he'd heard the gossips laughing amongst themselves about the mad God-botherers who battled invisible demons and lived together, praying and doing good deeds.

What had seemed hilarious or plain madness to his townsfolk, Stephen had found intriguing. A sign from Heaven.

He joined the Disciples of God within moments of meeting Lady Alice, bewitched by the Holy Mother's sincerity and obvious goodness.

Will wondered why the woman hadn't already married Stephen, for he seemed the perfect candidate for her wealth-acquiring scheme. Perhaps she knew he was so completely devoted to her that he'd accept her marrying other men before him. He was young enough to keep for a while, until she was ready to welcome him into her arms…

For the rest of the week, Will watched Stephen closely, taking note of his interactions with Lady Alice in particular, although he didn't think she lavished more attention on him than anyone else. Maybe she was going to leave the man alone for a while, enjoy the wealth she'd inherited from the other three men who'd died and then sink her claws into Stephen Drinkwater when she'd spent it all.

And, now that he was taking an interest, Scarlet did notice things that he hadn't before. While the Disciples drank weak beer which they brewed themselves, the Holy Mother had a stock of imported wines stored away in one of the chests within the south transept. Undoubtedly it was brought to her by Colwin, or perhaps David, both of whom made regular visits to the surrounding villages to collect supplies. Similarly, the Lady's chest contained exotic cheeses and choice cuts of salted meat, while the rest of the acolytes ate mostly bread, fish, and pottage which always seemed to be bubbling away over the cooking fire in the eastern end of St Joseph's where the altar had once been.

That kind of thing was not overtly ostentatious, and Will didn't feel greatly surprised that none of the Disciples grumbled about their meagre fare while the Holy Mother enjoyed the finest produce Yorkshire could offer at that time of the year. But, while the acolytes wore very simple, poor quality robes in what had once been white but was now a drab, uniform grey, Lady Alice bedecked herself in good quality material, tailored neatly although not extravagantly.

Furthermore, Will now noticed the jewels that sparkled on the necklaces and rings she wore and, while he was no expert in such things, he could tell by the size of gemstones that they must have been worth a very great deal.

The Lady always smelled far more pleasant than her followers too – of lavender, sandalwood, rose-petals, or even lemon – thanks to the scented oils she owned.

For a woman at the head of a sect which espoused the virtues of a frugal life, it seemed entirely incongruous, and more than a little unfair on her followers.

None complained, however; such was the depth of their devotion to the Lady.

And yet, Will did not think any of the Children of God were fools. It had been his initial assessment when John had told him about the strange sect, but now that he'd spent so much time with them, he'd found most of them to be intelligent, witty, and engaging companions.

It was just a shame that they'd allowed themselves to be taken in by Brother Colwin and Lady Alice.

On the Friday, the group were outside again, despite the biting wind and heavy grey clouds. It had been a week of hard toil for the acolytes, weaving many baskets which had been loaded, mostly by Will, onto the single ox-drawn cart the Disciples of God owned. Brothers Colwin and David had then taken turns driving the wagon to the various markets dotted around the area and sold them. On the Thursday they'd returned from Methley without a single basket, having sold them all, and that surprised Scarlet, for he hadn't expected the shaven-headed young men, with their soldierly bearing, to be the best at drawing in willing customers.

"This has been a very successful week, hasn't it?" Will felt a nudge and turned to see Margaret, grinning widely as she sat down next to him during a quick break from their work. "We've sold so many baskets and, even accounting for the materials, we must have put a nice bit of coin into the group's coffers, don't you think, Brother William? And it's all thanks to the Holy Mother's leadership."

Will held his face impassive, despite the urge to snort with laughter. The Holy Mother had not joined in with any of the work all week, instead spending her time walking in the grounds or, on the overcast, rainy days, staying in the back rooms of St Joseph, ostensibly praying, while her Disciples worked their fingers to the bone weaving and lifting and cooking and, of course, battling the Black Lords.

"Aye," Will said levelly. "It's been a successful week. What do you think we'll do with the money raised from the basket sales?"

Margaret's smile remained as wide as ever, a trait Will found endearingly innocent. She was an easy woman to get along with. "Oh," she replied, "the proceeds all go towards our food, drink, clothing, and maintaining the church here. The rest is given away to the poor and needy."

Will was not great with numbers, but even he knew that, with the number of baskets they'd made that week, there should have been a decent profit. He wondered which 'poor and needy' people their labours had benefited and knew it was a daft question. The only person profiting from the Disciples hard work was Lady Alice, surely.

"You really love the Holy Mother, don't you?" he asked.

"I do," she said proudly, bobbing her head up and down vigorously. "She is a great woman, sent here to help us do God's bidding. Don't you agree?"

"Oh, of course," Will agreed hastily. "A great woman. She's the reason I decided to join you, even though I must, unfortunately, spend my nights and some days at home in Methley taking care of my farm and my elderly mother. Perhaps one day I'll be able to commit fully to the Disciples."

"That would be wonderful, Brother William," Margaret said, so fervently that Scarlet believed she truly meant it. To her, the more people that followed Lady Alice the better. She stood up now, the sun appearing from behind a dark cloud just at that moment and forming a sort of halo behind her head. "I must get back to work now. It's time for the Holy Mother's massage – she gets terribly stiff in the afternoons, an unfortunate burden cast upon her by the Black Lords in revenge for her crusade against them."

She turned and walked off without waiting for a reply, which was just as well, for Scarlet wasn't sure he could make any reply to that statement without betraying his true thoughts. Fine food, imported wine, sparkling jewels, and a massage every day. Truly, Lady Alice had no need to do God's work to earn her rewards in heaven – she was already receiving them here on Earth!

As he rode home that night, Will's head whirled just as it always did after a day at St Joseph's. He rode to the north as usual, as if heading for Methley, before turning west for a time and turning south to join the road to Wakefield. Today, however, something caught his eye before he made the westward turn.

He stopped his horse mid-canter and jumped down to inspect the ground. The tracks of a wagon had caught his eye for, rather than following the main track of the road, they turned left, heading towards a patch of marshland, before rejoining the road further along.

There was no great mystery here, but it was such an inexplicable thing for a wagon driver to do that it caught Scarlet's attention. An ox wasn't the nimblest beast, and the danger of getting a wheel caught in the softer ground off-road, especially near marshland, would make most drivers wary of leaving the beaten track. What had caused this fellow to take such a course?

The sun was low in the sky and a cool wind made the air fresh as Will gazed out across the land. He could see nothing on the ground where the wagon had rested, although it was possible the driver had jumped down to urinate and it had soaked into the ground leaving no trace. But why take the wagon off the main track just for that? He gazed out into the marsh where reeds concealed who-knew what hungry wildlife at this time of the year, and then his eyes came to rest on something.

He walked forward a little, careful not to slip into the marsh for it was difficult to tell where the hard ground ended and the stagnant waters began. The thing he'd seen was difficult indeed to spot from here in the fading light, for its colour blended in almost invisibly with the drab surroundings. The rounded shape was at odds with the upright reeds though, and that's what had first drawn his attention. He knew now what it was – he'd spent enough time working with them during the past week after all.

A basket, bobbing gently in the water between half a dozen swaying rushes. And, now that he looked closer, he could see even more of them, tossed haphazardly into the marsh, where they'd undoubtedly have rotted away undiscovered, if it hadn't been for Will's curiosity over the unexpected path of the wagon. It wasn't the perfect hiding place, for the woven rushes the baskets had been made from floated naturally, so, although most of them were hidden by the reeds, Will estimated there to be at least twenty of the things dumped there.

He stared at the discarded baskets, feeling rage rising within him for there could be only one explanation for this: Brother Colwin had tossed them into the marsh because no-one had bought them.

But *why?*

Possibly the shaven-headed young man hadn't wanted to upset the other acolytes, by bringing them their labours home and telling them no-one had wanted them. But that just didn't strike Will as the truth.

No, these baskets could have been stored, and sold another day. The acolytes could have rested for a day, instead of pushing themselves close to exhaustion for the whole week. Will was furious now, as he thought of his own effort, loading the wagon – all for nothing. He pictured Colwin, smiling nastily as he threw basket after lovingly crafted basket into the marsh and, if Scarlet had cared little for the man before, he positively despised him now.

The way the unsuspecting Disciples of God were being treated by their two mentors was despicable, and that wasn't even taking into account the deaths of three men!

Shaking his head, and fingering the well-worn pommel of his longsword, Will made his way back to the road and mounted the waiting horse before riding hard for Wakefield.

God might be willing to turn a blind eye to the injustices occurring at St Joseph's but Will Scarlet would not stand for it any more. On the morrow there would be a reckoning, and 'Brother' Colwin would find out what it meant to stand on the battlefield against a true warrior.

CHAPTER SEVENTEEN

Little John hadn't been in Altofts village since the day he'd had to deal with the carpenter, Clibert, almost a year ago, but today he had another job there. For such a small place, he thought, it had more than its share of troublemakers who didn't like paying their fines.

His task had been simple enough – a pig-farmer, Jack, who lived on the southern outskirts of the village, had got into a dispute with a neighbouring family and damaged some of their property. He'd suffered a sore face for his troubles, when the two young sons that lived in the house came out to find Jack smashing one of their chicken coops. On top of that punishment, the unlucky pig-farmer had been fined four shillings but, believing he'd suffered enough already, he refused to pay it.

When the local bailiff came to collect the money he was chased by Jack, wielding a pitchfork. Of course, the bailiff would have been within his rights to draw his sword and kill the hot-headed fool, but, oddly enough, Jack was well-liked by most of the other villagers and killing him over an unpaid fine would have caused more trouble than it was worth.

So, John was sent, in the hope that his physical stature and reputation would be enough to persuade the man to pay up without any further hassles. And so it had turned out, for Jack was a great admirer of Robin Hood's exploits and held a deep respect for the part Little John had played in them. The two ended up beside one of the sties, sharing small mugs of beer as they discussed the finer points of pig-farming, troublesome neighbours, and the romance of life as an outlaw-prince.

Jack happily paid his fine over to John, saying it was worth it just to have spent some time speaking with Robin Hood's infamous right-hand man, and then the bailiff made his way back towards the main village in the hope of buying a proper mug of ale. Jack's offering might been the finest stuff in all England, but the stench of pig shit that pervaded the entire farm had rather soured John's experience.

He felt he'd earned a decent drink though, so, when he reached the village centre he paid the innkeeper to fill his aleskin and then took it along to Eustace the blacksmith.

"Hello, John," the burly metalworker said, nodding in welcome when he spotted the bailiff climbing down from his horse. "What's that you've got?" His eyes lit up when he realised what the item in John's hand was.

"You got time for a drink, Eustace?" the bailiff asked. "I mean, if you're too busy, I'll leave you to it—"

The smith's tongs had already been dropped with a metallic clatter and his heavy gloves were off before John could even finish his sentence. "Are you mad?" he demanded, grinning broadly. "I'm never too busy for a free drink. Come and join me here, it's nice and warm beside the furnace. You'll know that as well as I do, of course. Let me get some cups."

John nodded and walked to the side of the smithy where Eustace had a couple of stools sitting out, ready for occasions such as this.

"You on a job, or just here in Altofts to see my handsome face?"

John laughed. "It's always a delight to see you, my friend, but I had a fine to collect. From Jack, the pig-farmer."

It was Eustace's turn to laugh now, for Jack's recent adventures were well-known in the village. "Crazy bastard that one," he said. "Best company you could wish for in the alehouse on a November night though, notwithstanding the smell of manure that he seems to wear about him like a cloak all the time." He shook his head and gazed into the middle distance as if fondly remembering past drunken evenings with the pig-farmer. "Funny man, Jack, with a supply of stories that never seem to run out. Mad as a barrel of frogs though. You didn't hurt him, did you?" Eustace leaned forward, searching Little John for any signs of recent violence such as bloodied knuckles or facial bruising.

"Nah," the bailiff said, taking a sip of his ale. "He was quite friendly. Paid his fine and all's well."

The blacksmith muttered to himself, nodding in satisfaction. "That's good. He's a decent man. And those neighbours of his, well…I'd not like to live next to them either, put it that way."

The pair chatted amiably over the rest of the ale which was fresh enough but not particularly strong, and John was glad of that, since he still had to ride home to Wakefield. Eventually, just as he was about to say his farewells, the bailiff enquired after the men he'd fought with on his last visit to Altofts.

"Clibert and Fulke?" the smith spat on the grass next to him. "Still the same useless bastards as ever."

His face grew dark as he went on. "Some people are marked as troublemakers and it's not really a fair thing to say about them – Jack, for example. He's a good lad, essentially, just works a bit differently to the rest of us. But Clibert and Fulke, they're a real bad lot. I wouldn't be surprised if they've taken to robbing folk on the road and that's where their money comes from these days."

They sat in thoughtful silence, mulling over the societal mores that allowed certain people to go through life without really contributing much to their community, while others who worked hard and did their best to get on, were seen as figures of fun or even hate. John had known many men like Clibert and Fulke, for their kind had often tried to join the gangs he was part of during his days as an outlaw.

"There's something really sinister about that whoreson Clibert," the blacksmith opined quietly. "That burn mark under his eye always makes me curious—" He broke off, seeing John staring at him from beneath furrowed brows. Before he could say anything else, the bailiff had got to his feet, shoved the stopper back into his aleskin and, with hardly a word of farewell, was striding towards his horse.

"What's going on?" Eustace called in bemusement. "Where are you going? God's blood, bailiff, you're as mad as Jack!"

"Clibert lives at the end of the road, doesn't he?" John asked, unclipping his staff from his horse's saddle and turning back to the smith. "One of the last houses in the village?"

"Aye, second from the end," Eustace confirmed. "You can't miss it. He's a carpenter but the place is falling to ruin. You'll know it when you see it. But why do you ask? And do you want me to come with you?" This final question was shouted, for Little John's long stride was already carrying him along the road, northwards, towards Clibert's home.

"No, I'm just going to talk with him," he shouted over his shoulder, but there was a distinct emphasis placed on the word *talk* and Eustace smiled wryly and retrieved his dropped gloves before returning to his work at the forge.

It didn't take John long to reach his destination, and he noted with disgust that Eustace's description of the place was accurate. The shutters were firmly attached to their hinges, but the wood was rotten in places, having not seen a coat of paint in years. The door looked similarly flimsy, which surprised the bailiff. Given how many people Clibert got on the wrong side of, John would have expected him to at least have a secure door to keep them out if they came looking for him.

He stood before the rotten door, eyeing it thoughtfully for a moment, then, with a shrug and a wicked smile, he leaned back and slammed his boot against the wood. As he'd hoped, the whole lower section exploded in a satisfying mess of damp splinters and, without waiting for an invitation, he pushed the remaining door open, bent down, and strode into the gloomy little hovel.

"What the f—"

Clibert came at him, aiming a punch at his neck, for he wasn't tall enough to reach John's face with any power. Not that he had any chance of landing the blow anyway.

John's staff came up, batting Clibert's fist aside, and then the bailiff hammered his knee into his opponent's midriff, dropping him like a stone.

A second man was in the house – gap-toothed Fulke. He stared at the towering bailiff, who glared back at him in a way that promised terrible violence to any who stood in his way, and Fulke decided his friendship with Clibert wasn't worth having his nose broken again. He very slowly edged towards the wrecked door, then, with a strangely polite nod of farewell, ran off down the street as fast as his legs would take him.

"For God's sake," the downed man gasped in a tortured, nasal tone. "What's the matter with you, bailiff? I've done nothing wrong." He had to draw in another painful breath before he could continue. "What d'you think you're doing, smashing my door like that, and assaulting me?"

In reply, John bent down, grabbed Clibert by the front of his grimy tunic, and hauled him effortlessly up, before tossing him onto a stool. This didn't work out quite as he'd intended, for Clibert fell off immediately, landing on his back with his legs in the air like a woodlouse turned upside down by a vindictive child.

"Oh, get up you oaf," John growled, once again lifting the protesting man and depositing him, a little more carefully this time, onto the stool again.

"What the hell's this all about?" Clibert whined, still not quite able to breathe properly. "You can't just..." He trailed off, noting John's stare, and self-consciously touched the burn mark that had been on his cheek for years now. "What do you want from me, Little John?"

"I want you to tell me everything you know about the Disciples of God, Clibert," the bailiff replied, lifting his enormous quarterstaff and placing the butt on the stool, directly between the terrified carpenter's legs. "And if I don't think you're telling me the truth, trust me – you'll never need to pay for a woman again."

CHAPTER EIGHTEEN

Little John shook his head in wonder, staring at the cowering form before him. In the end, he hadn't needed to crack Clibert's skull, or balls, with his quarterstaff – the man was not the bravest and he knew very well that John wasn't playing. When the bailiff threatened violence, someone *would* get hurt – it was a well-known fact throughout northern England. So Clibert spoke up readily enough when John started questioning him.

"You were working with the Disciples of God," the bailiff said, in a tone that brooked no disagreement. "I've been told by people in different counties that a barber-surgeon with a burn beneath their eye diagnosed Henry of Castellford and Brother Morris with some terrible illness that would kill them."

It wasn't exactly true, but it was close enough. Clibert opened his mouth to deny the accusation, but one look at John's face changed his mind. The man knew he'd been caught out, and his jaw closed again as the bailiff continued.

"You were the supposed 'barber-surgeon', Clibert. And, when the men took their own lives, Lady Alice de Staynton rewarded you. Which explains that heavy purse of money you had on you that first day I came to collect your fine and knocked you out. I always knew there was too much there for it have simply been payment for clearing some junk out of the church."

Again, Clibert remained silent.

"It was you, wasn't it?" the bailiff shouted, pushing his quarterstaff forward so it pressed against Clibert's manhood. "You were the 'barber-surgeon'."

"Aye, it was me!" the frightened man confessed. "All I did was act like I knew what I was doing, examine their heads, and tell them they were ill. Just like the Holy Mother told me to do. I didn't have much choice."

"What are you talking about," John demanded. "No one forced you to drive those men to their deaths. You were paid to do it."

"That big Disciple," Clibert muttered, looking down at the floor. "With the shaved head. He made it clear I'd better do as they said, or I'd be sorry." He looked up again, meeting John's hard eyes. "He's a scary man, that one."

"So am I," John growled.

"Aye, you are," Clibert returned. "But you weren't there, and he was."

"That doesn't surprise me," the bailiff said. "I knew that bastard was involved all along." He drew back his staff, allowing his prisoner to relax just a little as he continued to question him. "What about your slow-witted friend, Fulke? He's never far away when you're around. What part did he play in all this?"

Clibert waved a hand dismissively. "He had nothing to do with it. He's an idiot."

John gazed at him, trying to gauge the truthfulness of his claim. "You're right," he agreed. "Anyone that hangs around with you is indeed an idiot," he muttered. No one had mentioned the 'barber-surgeon' having a gap-toothed companion, however, so he let the matter rest there for now.

Clibert just stared at him sullenly.

"What amazes me the most," said John, shaking his head. "Is the fact anyone believed that you – you! – were a barber surgeon!" He laughed humourlessly. "I, personally, find it hard to believe you can dress yourself in the morning, never mind perform surgery on anyone."

"It's the woman," Clibert muttered, cowed, and embarrassed to have admitted his part in Lady Alice's scheme so easily. "She has all those men in her sect wrapped around her little finger. They'd have believed I'd come down from the moon if she told them it was true."

"*I'd* believe you came down from the moon," John snorted. "Before I accepted the fact that you were a barber surgeon."

"Aye, all right," Clibert gurned, staring up at the bailiff irritably. "You've had your fun. Now can you leave me alone? I've things to do."

"I can imagine," John retorted. "Heading to the alehouse for a few drinks, before making your way to St Joseph's to warn the Holy Mother that I'll be coming for her. I don't think so. Get up." He gestured with the butt of his staff and Clibert did as he was commanded.

"What now?" the carpenter demanded. "I haven't actually broken any laws, have I? You can't arrest me."

John shrugged his great shoulders and grasped Clibert by the arm, leading him towards the broken door. "I've no idea about what laws you might have broken," he admitted. "Perhaps you're right and you've not broken any. But I'm not having you warning Lady Alice that I'm onto her, so…walk."

"Where to?"

"Altofts has a guild hall, doesn't it? That'll do."

"You can't lock me up," Clibert protested, but John still had a firm grip on his arm and squeezed it painfully now.

"I can do what I like," the bailiff said. "You played a part in the deaths of at least two men, and it wouldn't surprise me at all if you were there at old Elias's house in Wakefield the night he was murdered." He watched his captive's face as he spoke and noticed the tell-tale shifting of Clibert's eyes as the accusation was made. "I knew it. You really are a piece of work. Well, this time I'm going to see you get what you deserve, you useless old sot."

They walked along the road, drawing the attention of everyone they passed until there was a crowd of villagers watching them. Children laughed excitedly, and Eustace the blacksmith came hurrying out as they went by his forge.

"I'm taking him to the guildhall," John told the burly man. "I'd be grateful if you and Geoffrey, the headman, can make sure he doesn't escape."

Eustace nodded grimly. "We'll make sure of it, John. How long should we keep him there? Will there be soldiers coming from Nottingham to take him away?"

"I'm not sure yet, my friend. Just keep him locked up and alive until I come back for him, eh? I'll need his testimony when all this comes to a head."

At that moment the village headman appeared, and John gladly gave possession of his prisoner over to him, knowing Eustace would make sure Clibert didn't try to make a run for it.

"Thank you," the bailiff said. "I'll fill you in on everything that's been happening another time. For now, I should be going, before it gets dark. Looks like I'll have a busy day tomorrow, for every moment wasted could mean this one's accomplices getting further away, if they get word that I'm coming for them."

With that, John hurried to his horse, climbed into the saddle, and kicked his heels in, galloping hard towards Wakefield, for he knew he'd need help arresting Lady Alice. The Disciples of God would surely not let her be taken without a fight...

CHAPTER NINETEEN

"So now we have a witness," Friar Tuck said, nodding in satisfaction before taking another sip of his ale.

"Aye, assuming the carpenter repeats his story in front of the sheriff," Will noted uncertainly. "I wouldn't be surprised if the Disciples get to him, and he claims John made it all up and he's as innocent as a newborn lamb."

They were gathered in Little John's house again, with a skin of ale which Tuck had brought himself, not wishing to impose too much on Amber's hospitality. She had, of course, laughed and told him not to be foolish while furnishing them with bread and sweetmeats and then sitting down near the window with her sewing, making the most of the light before the sun went down.

"I doubt it," John said. "He's safely locked away in Altofts where the Disciples can't reach him, unless they were to mount a full-scale attack, and that would just draw even more attention to themselves. Besides, they don't know he's informed on them yet – they've no reason to go after him."

They mulled over John's revelation that a simple carpenter from the nearby village had been the so-called 'barber-surgeon' who'd delivered the damning diagnoses to the two men who'd taken their own lives.

"That was a fine piece of deduction," Tuck said, smiling proudly at the bailiff. "To figure out who he was and getting him to confess."

"Aye, and you were right about Colwin all along," Will said, recounting his own discovery of the abandoned baskets and what he believed it meant.

"I think our course is set, then," the friar said, leaning back and rubbing his full belly. "Tomorrow we go to St Joseph's and arrest Lady Alice."

John blew out a deep breath and rolled his head from side to side, making the joints in his neck crack audibly. "Are you sure, Tuck?" he asked. "Do we really have enough now to prove what she's been up to?"

"We have proof enough," the friar replied. "I don't know what else we can do. If we wait any longer to find more evidence the woman will move onto another victim. I think we need to stop her now – she's claimed enough victims."

"To be honest," Will broke in. "I don't think she's ready to make her next move yet. Her obvious target will be Stephen Drinkwater, but I've not seen any evidence of her being any friendlier to him than anyone else."

"That may be so," Tuck said ruefully. "But how long did it take her to wed poor Elias and then take his fortune? Mere weeks. She moves fast, Will, and if this Drinkwater fellow is already enamoured with her, he's at great risk, I believe."

"Fair enough," Scarlet shrugged. "I've had enough of St bloody Joseph's anyway. The sooner we arrest Lady Alice and Colwin the better."

"What will happen to the rest of the Disciples?" a voice asked from the corner, and the three men turned to look at Amber. "I mean, when their leaders are gone. Will they be all right?"

John, Tuck, and Will looked at one another in surprise. Not one of them had even thought about the consequences of Lady Alice being found guilty of the crimes they believed her to have perpetrated.

"I, well, I suppose St Joseph's will be seized by the crown," Tuck said. "And the Disciples will be put out."

"I thought those people were vulnerable," Amber said, eyes fixed on her sewing but her tone no less accusatory for that. "Driving them out of their home, without anyone to lead them…Doesn't seem right, does it?"

"What are we supposed to do?" John asked his wife. "We don't make up the laws. You're not suggesting we just let Lady Alice continue to do what she's been doing up until now? She's had a hand in killing three innocent men, and that's just the ones we know about! I think it's safe to say she's done away with more, before the Disciples came into our part of the world."

"Oh, I think you need to stop her, of course," Amber said, nodding as her fingers worked nimbly with her needle and thread. "But maybe there's a way to remove her, without her followers suffering too."

"Like what?" Will demanded. "Don't get me wrong, I've spent a lot of time with those people lately, and they're kind and gentle, most of them. I just don't see a way to help them here. How can we?"

"I don't know," Amber admitted. "But those poor acolytes don't deserve to suffer because their leader is a devil."

The men knew John's wife was right, but there was nothing they could do about it. The Disciples of God had thrown their lot in with Lady Alice de Staynton and, when she was brought down, they would fall with her. That was how life worked out sometimes, as harsh as it was.

There was a thoughtful silence in the room for a long time but, eventually, John said, "Our course is set anyway, regardless of the consequences. We go to St Joseph's tomorrow and I arrest Lady Alice in as peaceful a manner as possible. Agreed?"

Tuck and Will both nodded, and, with that, any feelings of pleasure in the evening evaporated, like steam from a boiling cauldron, and the pair stood up to go home, not looking forward to the morrow at all.

"Tell me," Amber asked, watching them as they made to leave. "Is the Lady Alice very beautiful?"

After a moment's pause, Tuck replied, diplomatically, "You know that beauty is in the eye of the beholder."

Scarlet however was, as usual, more direct. "No," he said bluntly. "She's short and plump and not very handsome at all."

Amber's gaze returned to her sewing as Little John closed and bolted the door behind their visitors and she muttered, to herself more than anyone else, "Just as well, eh? Imagine how many more followers she'd have if she was."

* * *

The figure knew how to stick to the shadows, moving with almost preternatural silence in the dark, undetected by those who lay sleeping peacefully in the room around him. His hand caressed the pommel of his sword, a movement that had become instinctive over the years for he had suffered a hard life, despite his relative youth.

His feet were bare, as he feared his boots would have seemed loud in the still of the night, tapping against the cold flagstones the church had been floored with. He shivered; autumn seemed to have fled before winter already and, since the fire in the chancel had burned low, the stained-glass windows were showing a glittering coat of frost, even on the inside.

A heavy snore, almost a choking, halted him in his tracks and he looked at the Disciples on their bedrolls, but it was just one of the older men. The figure waited for a second, until all grew calm again, and then walked on, into the vestry, where Brother Morris had taken his own life. Then, he lifted aside a tapestry on the eastern side of the room, revealing a low, narrow door, which he opened and passed through.

This next section of the church was most unusual. A slender corridor ran from the vestry, around a corner to a small, windowless chamber located behind the chancel wall. It was rumoured that the nobleman who'd paid for St Joseph's to be built generations before had incorporated this room into the plan so the priest would have somewhere to hide in the event of a raid by marauding Vikings. The story was probably apocryphal for the chamber was no great secret – anyone looking towards the chancel from inside the main body of the church would notice there were no windows there. But if one stood outside and looked at the eastern wall, they couldn't help but notice the two small, stained-glass windows and wonder what room they looked in upon.

Whatever the truth of the matter, it wasn't important to the figure walking along the corridor now.

He carried no light, but his eyes were well adjusted to the dark, and the moonlight coming through the small window in the vestry was just enough to let him see the heavy door standing between him and his destination. Beneath it, he could see a sliver of orange spilling out and he knew a candle was lit within the 'secret' chamber.

The Holy Mother's chamber.

Through that door was the one room where the acolytes were not allowed to go – the place where Lady Alice stored her own private documents, and also where she sometimes slept. Alone.

Or at least that was what she told her Disciples and, even during the short time when she'd been married to Brother Elias, he'd slept in the main body of the church, while she spent her nights here, in the quarters on the other side of the door which the silent figure now stopped in front of, listening.

At first, he heard nothing, but then, through the thick, sturdy oak, there came the sound of soft laughter. This might not have been that strange, had it not been for the fact it was a man's laugh. Lady Alice had a nocturnal visitor to her private bedchamber.

The eavesdropper pressed his head against the door, listening intently, yet terrified he'd be discovered. He had to know what was happening within the candlelit room though.

There was more muffled laughter, this time from both the man and Lady Alice, as they shared some joke. And then there was a new sound – one not particularly familiar to the lurker at the threshold, yet quite unmistakeable – of a woman squealing with delight. It wasn't very loud, as if the person making it didn't want anyone outside the locked room to notice it, but the eavesdropper could hear it with agonizing clarity through the wood his ear was pressed against.

The grunting, which reminded the listener of animals – pigs, perhaps – began then, and it was now devastatingly obvious what was happening inside Lady Alice's bedchamber.

Shock, hurt, confusion, and a myriad other emotions beset the watcher at the door and he reeled away, head spinning, pressing his back against the corridor wall, feeling its coolness and clinging to it with sweating palms as if it might anchor him to safe, reliable, reality once more.

And then, fearing discovery, he half ran, half staggered, back through the vestry and into the nave, where he found his sleeping pallet and lay down, tears streaking his face. He wished sleep would take him into its merciful oblivion but never before had he felt so awake and all he could do was lie in the dark, reliving the terrible moments that had changed his life – changed *him* – forever.

A short time later he heard soft footsteps approaching and a tall, shaven-headed figure was revealed in the blue moonlight streaming through the church's windows. Oblivious to the eyes watching him, the man moved carefully past the Disciples' sleeping bodies and lay down on his own rough bed where, within moments, clearly exhausted from his exertions within the Holy Mother's chamber, he fell fast asleep.

While the watcher in the dark looked on in righteous disgust, wondering how he could carry on living in this hateful world.

CHAPTER TWENTY

The next day brought a thick fog, and Will Scarlet was glad of it, for it meant he could wear a heavy cloak and that would hide the vest of chainmail he'd put on. If there was going to be a fight with Colwin, David, and the Black-Lords-knew who else, he wanted to be well prepared for it.

Riding into the centre of Wakefield he met Little John and Tuck, already mounted and ready to go. John looked even bigger than usual thanks to the mail he wore beneath his own cloak and, unusually, he had his longbow with him, and at least half a dozen arrows tucked into his belt.

The jovial friar looked much the same as he always did, but Will knew from long experience that Tuck could be counted on in even the most brutal and bloody of fights, despite his potbelly and ready smile.

They rode together towards St Joseph's, huddling into their cloaks against the cold, but about half a mile from the church they left the main road, finding a spot well hidden by trees and undergrowth, reined in their horses and looked at one another.

"I think I should go on ahead," Scarlet suggested. "See how things stand. Maybe Colwin and David have already travelled to market on the wagon and we can quickly ride in and take Lady Alice into custody without any need for a fight."

John nodded. "All right, that sounds sensible. Just be careful though, Will. If word has reached them that I arrested Clibert for his part in all this, they might be expecting someone to come looking for the Holy Mother."

"They won't think it'll be me though," Scarlet protested.

"Maybe not," Tuck said. "But they might be on edge and you are, after all, still not fully one of their group. You're an outsider, living outwith the community, and you have been asking the acolytes a lot of questions in the past couple of weeks. That could make the Lady and her lackeys suspicious of you."

"Plus, Colwin has already had a run in with you." John dismounted and pegged his horse to the ground, giving its neck a reassuring rub before turning to Will again. "Just be careful, old friend. We'll walk to the church at your back, but I don't want to get there and find you already dead."

Will smiled. "Don't worry about me, lads. I'll be fine." He patted his sword hilt and turned his horse back towards the road. "Don't take too long to come though. The sooner we can get this over with the better." With that he spurred the mount on and disappeared amongst the foliage, the sound of thundering hooves reaching them moments later and then fading into the distance as he rode to St Joseph's.

"You heard him," John said to Tuck. "Let's go. Try and keep up!"

With the friar muttering at his back, the bailiff began striding through the trees towards the church, wondering what they'd find when they got there, and praying no one else was dead because of Lady Alice de Staynton by the time the sun set in the western sky.

* * *

Will dismounted and, after making sure his horse was settled and watered, walked inside the church. The fog had started to lift as the sun rose higher and began to burn it away, but it was still damp out and there was no sign of any acolytes working in the grounds.

"Good morning, Brother William."

Stephen Drinkwater greeted him warmly, looking up from his cross-legged position on the floor inside St Joseph's. The old man was weaving yet another basket, as were the other Disciples who were in the church.

Will counted them, surprised to see only a few other people working within the nave. There was no sign of Lady Alice, or Brothers Colwin or David, and, for an instant, Will wondered if they really had been given word of Little John's arrest of Clibert, and decided to simply ride off before the law could come looking for them.

Yet Stephen looked relaxed and peaceful, despite his old fingers being entirely unsuited to the task of weaving, and so did the rest of the acolytes seated on the floor. The fire in the chancel was lit, warming some pottage or broth in the cauldron over it as usual, and it lent the air a cosy, homely ambience quite at odds with the damp morning outside.

"Where is everyone?" Scarlet asked nonchalantly, gathering completed baskets and lifting them across to the doorway, ready to be taken out to the wagon when it was brought around. "Gone off to one of the nearby villages already?"

"Some of them, yes," Stephen replied without looking up from his work. His brow was furrowed and he looked close to exploding with exasperation as he attempted to feed the end of his rushes through a hole that seemed much too small to take them and he didn't expand on his reply. Neither did any of the other Disciples.

They took their work so seriously, Scarlet thought, with a surge of anger as he remembered the pile of baskets, floating in the marshes not a mile away from where their oblivious creators were diligently crafting even more. At least their willingness to work hard would stand them in good stead, he mused, when the Holy Mother was brought to account for her crimes and they were forced to make a new life for themselves without her to guide them.

He finished lifting the baskets and looked at the acolytes. They were all quiet, placid types, he knew – they might raise their eyebrows if he did something unusual, but he didn't believe they would question him, never mind try to stop him, if he snooped around a bit.

With that in mind, he walked confidently towards the rear of the church and, without a backwards glance, opened the door to the vestry and went through, closing it behind himself. Instinctively, he touched the pommel of his sword, double-checking it was still safely within its scabbard, just in case some hidden foe was in the small room. He gave thanks to God that this strange sect would not only allow its members to carry deadly weapons, but actually encourage it. Black Lords be damned, he thought, the only enemies I need to fear here are Colwin and David.

The room was empty however and, for a moment, he thought about searching for something they could use against Lady Alice – some piece of evidence, hidden away, that might prove her part in the deaths of the three men. He had no idea what to look for though, and, besides, it was highly unlikely the woman would be so stupid as to leave anything incriminating lying around here, in the unlocked room.

Or would she? His eye was caught by something, a glint of metal in the meagre light coming through the small window and he bent down to draw out a small chest from beneath a table. A low whistle escaped his lips as he took in the contents of the chest: jewellery. There were gold and silver chains along with necklaces, brooches with precious gems inset, and rings. Scarlet didn't know much about such trinkets, but he knew this lot was worth a fortune. He fished out one small piece, a brooch with a green stone in it, recognising it as one Sister Margaret had been wearing the first day he'd met her. No doubt it, along with everything else collected in the chest, had been gifted to the Lady Alice by Margaret and her fellow Disciples, desperate to please their manipulative Holy Mother.

Unfortunately, however, it didn't prove any crime had been committed.

He stood there wondering what to do next. Should he go back to Tuck and John and tell them there was no sign of their prey? He opened the door to the nave just a crack, peering out, checking none of the acolytes had grown curious and was coming to see what he was up to, but they were all still working away in silence.

For spiritual people, he thought bitterly, they don't really have much spirit.

He shut the door silently again and took a deep breath, steeling himself. He couldn't go back to John and Tuck yet – there was still one room he hadn't looked in: Lady Alice's chamber.

It was the one part of the church Will had never been in. He knew the tapestry—a wonderfully woven piece which depicted a vivid hunting scene—concealed a door leading to another room, for he'd been told about it not long after he'd 'joined' the Disciples of God. The acolytes were not allowed in there though, for it was the Holy Mother's sacred retreat, where she could rest and recuperate after battling Black Lords. She needed such a sanctuary for, as their leader, she felt the pain of their struggles the most.

Ridiculous bloody lies, Scarlet thought angrily, drawing back the tapestry and, finding the door behind it unlocked. He peered into the narrow, gloomy corridor, then, hearing and seeing no-one, he walked quickly along and pushed open the door that led into the off-limits bedchamber. Thankfully, the pair of stained-glass windows offered plenty of light after the claustrophobic darkness of the adjoining corridor.

He drew his sword and stepped into the cramped little room, noting the fine wooden bed that was its centrepiece. No bundle of straw on the floor for Lady Alice de Staynton, oh no, she slept soundly on—

There was a noise to his side, and he turned just in time to see a fist coming towards his face. He wasn't fast enough to dodge it though, and, as it cannoned against his cheek, lights exploded in his vision and he stumbled to the side, fighting desperately to keep his feet. If he fell, he knew he was as good as dead.

He tried to swing his sword, to keep his assailant at bay, but the man was already upon him, hammering his fists and knees into him, and now Scarlet did collapse onto the stone floor, for his attacker was tall and the weight of his body was too much to stand against in his injured state.

"You bastard! This is all your fault! You and your damn friends!"

The ferocity of the blows, and the confusing, screamed words, served to disorientate Will, who'd dropped his sword and felt a momentary surge of panic coursing through him. What was this madman shouting about? What was his fault? What friends? There was no way the man had mistaken him for someone else, for, although the violence had exploded in the blink of an eye, Will recognised his attacker: Brother Colwin.

The crazed Disciple fell on top of him, grasping him by the throat with both hands, pressing down with terrific force. Will struggled but he was weakened and in a terrible position that allowed him to gain no purchase on his attacker's wrists, or even lever his body into a better place. He was trapped, and he was passing out, and all he could think as he stared in Colwin's crazed eyes was that they'd terribly underestimated the young man.

The pressure suddenly lessened around Will's throat, allowing him to suck in a breath. He tried to aim a punch at Brother Colwin but he didn't have the strength. It didn't matter though, for the shaven-headed young Disciple leaned back, taking his hands away completely, and then his face screwed up and he stood, sobbing as he looked down at Scarlet.

The ferocity of the attack might have faded for now, but the light of madness was still in Colwin's eyes, and Will rolled onto his side, desperately trying to get to his feet that he might defend himself against whatever was about to happen next.

"This is all your fault," Colwin said, but he sounded terribly sad now, rather than murderous, and Will, coughing and struggling to breathe, looked up at him. "You, and the fat friar, and the scruffy bailiff…"

"What…" Scarlet managed to push himself onto his hands and knees but no further. "What are you talking about, you madman? What's my fault?"

Colwin turned away and stepped towards Lady Alice's bed. He stood in front of it, staring down at the embroidered blankets illuminated by the colourful sunlight coming through the stained-glass windows. There were tears in his eyes and apparently he did not fear Will now that his own righteous fury had passed. "I was outside the bailiff's house the other night you know." Still the acolyte stared at the bed, and seemed to be lost in a strange daydream, talking more for his own benefit than Scarlet's. "I knew you weren't who you claimed to be. 'William of Clipston'. Pfft." Now he did turn his head to look at the man he'd been trying to murder just moments before. "I followed you when you rode home that day. And I followed you when you met the friar and John Little at the bailiff's house. I hid outside and listened to what you were all saying, about us and about the Holy Mother."

Will managed to grasp his sword and draw it towards himself, but Brother Colwin either didn't register the steel blade scraping across the flagstones, or simply didn't care.

"I couldn't believe it," the acolyte went on. "I thought you were mad, or just troublemakers who didn't agree with our mission to stop the Black Lords and refused to see the good in what we've built here."

"Good?" Will demanded in a harsh, strangled tone. "Making people work, only to throw away the fruit of their labours? How is that good? And that's before we even mention the men you've killed."

Colwin turned now and stared at him in bemusement but it wasn't the murder accusation that had caught his interest. "Throw away work? What are you talking about now? More lies?"

"The baskets," Will said. "You're not the only one that can follow tracks. I saw the baskets the other Disciples had made, all thrown away into the marsh. Discarded like rubbish after the men and women had worked their fingers to the bone on them. All so you and your *Holy Mother* can keep them beavering away like docile little beasts of burden, too busy to ever ask questions about what's really going on here."

Colwin's face twisted in confusion. "I don't know what you're talking about, you old fool. I never threw away any baskets – Brother David sold them all in Nostell and Croftun."

They stared at one another in silence then, Will not seeing any point in arguing the matter further given he could barely breathe, never mind talk.

Colwin's bemused look turned suddenly to one of understanding, almost as if some revelation had struck him like a beam of light from heaven, and he growled, "Brother David." He looked at Will and seemed almost excited now. "You and your friends believed I was in league with the Holy Mother, didn't you? But you're wrong." His anger returned now, making his eyes blaze as he pointed towards the bed. "It's not me – it's David. I heard them together here, last night."

Will frowned. "'Heard them'? You have an unhealthy habit of sneaking about, spying on people, don't you? What d'you mean you, 'heard them'?"

"They were rutting like animals!" Colwin shouted, striking the blankets with his fist and suddenly Will understood the young Disciple's rage.

"And then you knew that the Holy Mother had been lying to you all along. She wanted David, not you."

Colwin's brow furrowed, as if he were dealing with an imbecile. "You think I was jealous of their nocturnal lust? Then you haven't understood our sect at all." He spoke slowly now, moving his hands around in the air as if using them to punctuate his words. "We value virginity above all else. Or at least, chastity. Even those Disciples who are married do not sleep together – they love one another as they would their parents or siblings. *That* is what the Holy Mother teaches us, yet she does not follow her own rules!"

No wonder the young acolyte was furious, Will thought – everything he believed in had turned out to be a sham. Lady Alice was no bastion of morality, of chastity. Colwin had overheard Scarlet, Tuck, and John discussing her murderous schemes, and then he'd discovered she was enjoying night-time debaucheries with Brother David. It was quite obvious Colwin was in love with the woman but had accepted he could never have her, physically, for it was against their holy vows.

Yet, all along, his quiet friend, David, was enjoying those same, unattainable pleasures Colwin wanted so much.

Will felt sorry for the naïve, confused young acolyte now, for the bottom had fallen out of his world completely and his life was left in tatters. The woman Colwin thought he loved no longer existed for him – she was as good as dead, and his grief had been given a conduit in his violent assault on Will. It was all terribly sad – another man's life ruined by Lady Alice de Staynton's voracious appetite for power – but there were more pressing matters to deal with at that moment.

"Where is she?" Will demanded. "You know what she is now. What she's been doing. We have to stop her, before she drives any more men to their deaths."

Colwin sat down heavily on the bed, as if all the fight had gone from him and nothing mattered any more. "She went to Castellford—there's a little island where the River Aire meets the Calder."

"I know it," Scarlet nodded.

"She said it would be a nice, sunny day, perfect for a boat ride and picnic on the island." Brother Colwin shook his head. "I don't know why you and your friends keep saying Lady Alice drives men to their deaths. Aye, it's true some of the men in our group have died recently but, if it's true that she was the cause of their deaths, I have to tell you: Female disciples have taken their own lives over the past couple of years as well."

That surprised Will, but then, thinking about it, it made sense. *All* the Disciples of God were besotted with Lady Alice, why should it only be men who were willing to give up their lives if they thought that's what she wanted? The idea had not crossed his mind until now, but it wasn't hard to believe.

"It doesn't matter right now," he told Colwin, sliding his sword back into its sheath. "That will all come out at her trial, I'm sure. Right now, we need to arrest her." He turned to leave the bedchamber, to return to his friends waiting outside, but Colwin called to him as he went through the door.

"It *does* matter, Brother William. You see, the Holy Mother didn't just go to the river with David. She took Margaret and Denise."

Scarlet stopped dead and turned back to see Colwin still on the bed, with his head in his hands.

"Margaret? So what?"

"So what?" Colwin cried, looking up in anguish. "Sister Margaret is the wealthiest member of our sect! Did your snooping not reveal that fact? If you really believe Lady Alice is doing away with people so she can get her hands on their fortune, Margaret would be the ideal target."

Shrugging, Will began to move again. It didn't really make any difference – they had enough witnesses to prove Lady Alice's wrongdoing. "We're going to arrest her right now," he shouted back along the corridor as he reached the nave. "It doesn't matter who's on the little boat trip with her."

"I sincerely hope you're right, 'Brother William'," Colwin shouted after him. "Because I know that neither Margaret nor her daughter can swim!"

CHAPTER TWENTY-ONE

"By God, what the hell happened to you?" Little John stared at Scarlet in amazement when he burst out of the church's great doors, bruised and bloodstained. "Where are you going?" This last question was shouted, for the battered man had mounted his horse and was already guiding it hastily towards the main road.

"Come on!" Scarlet shouted over his shoulder. "We need to get to Castellford as quickly as possible, before someone else dies. Hurry, I'll explain on the way."

Cursing loudly, Tuck and John were forced to run back the way they'd just come, to the stand of trees where they'd left their own horses. Tuck's grey robes flew behind him as he hurried, red-faced, behind the giant bailiff, whose long legs ate up the ground with comparative ease. Scarlet looked back at them but he was in no mood to make light of the pair's appearance, something Tuck noted instantly, for he was expecting the usual mockery about his lack of grace and knew it was a bad sign when it didn't come.

It seemed to take them forever to make it back to the waiting horses, and the friar was blowing heavily so John helped him, none too gently, up into the saddle, before mounting his own mare. Scarlet watched them impatiently and then kicked his heels in and led them at a gallop to the east, trees, bushes and even one startled farmer passing in a blur.

Little John pushed his mare hard until it was beside Scarlet's charging animal and shouted to him. "What happened in the church, Will? And why this mad ride to Castellford?"

"Brother Colwin attacked me," Scarlet replied, voice carrying backwards in the wind to Tuck who brought up the rear of their small party. "We were wrong about him all along – he's not part of Lady Alice's mad schemes. Quite the opposite."

"Then why did he attack you?" Tuck demanded. "Looks like he did a good job of it too; you're a mess, Will!"

Scarlet couldn't make out the friar's words over the air rushing past them but he guessed his friend's question, and called a loud reply. "I'll explain it all later. For now, the Holy Mother's taken two of the female Disciples to the River Aire for a boating trip. I fear she's going to drown them."

"Why?" John cried.

"They're rich," was Will Scarlet's short, shouted explanation and it was enough. Tuck and John's imaginations filled in the blanks and asked no more questions as their horses carried them through the countryside of northern England.

The journey to Castellford was only about five miles but the road wasn't in good condition and they found their progress slowed in places. Scarlet mentally kicked himself as they rode at breakneck speed through another tiny hamlet, scattering squawking hens in their wake and drawing the ire of an old woman who shook her fist at their rapidly retreating backs. *Why did we assume Lady Alice would only target men?* It had seemed a logical conclusion at the time but now…He pictured Margaret, ubiquitous smile in place, with her daughter Denise by her side, and then his brain formed an image of the pair lying face down and unmoving in the river.

Of course, there would be a funeral for them, with Lady Alice leading the tearful tributes and then, a few days later would come the revelation that Sister Margaret had recently changed her will, bequeathing all her wealth and property to the Disciples of God and their charismatic Holy Mother.

"She's pure evil," Scarlet muttered to himself as his horse galloped around a corner and there at last, not half a mile distant, was the River Aire with its little, tree-filled island sitting serenely in the middle. "That's it," he called to his companions. "Look for a boat; they'd have paid to borrow one in Castellford."

They spurred their mounts for one last push, coming to the water's edge moments later but, to their frustration, there was no sign of a boat, Lady Alice, or anyone else. The only living thing they could see was a heron, which stood motionless on the opposite bank of the river, patiently waiting for prey.

"They're not here," John growled in frustration. "Now what? This river runs for miles, we could spend all day riding along it before we found them."

"Assuming they even came here in the first place," Tuck added, turning to Scarlet with a frown. "Brother Colwin could have sent you here to get us out of the way, while he and Lady Alice make their escape."

Scarlet stared at the dark, flowing waters of the Aire, knuckles white as he gripped his horse's reins. "I don't think so," he said at last, gently kicking his heels in and urging the animal to walk on. "He was beside himself with righteous anger. I'm sure he was telling the truth, although I suppose it's possible the Lady went somewhere else for their boat trip—"

From the far end of the little island there came a sudden scream, followed by an almighty splash and the three horsemen stopped, listening. And then Scarlet shouted, "Come on, they're behind the trees!" and kicked his mount into a gallop once more.

"Help! Help me—" The voice was unmistakably that of a girl, and her cries were cut off because, as Scarlet saw as the end of the small island finally came into sight, her head had gone under the water.

"Denise," he muttered, staring in horror at the sight before them.

The twelve-year-old was floundering ineffectually in the river, her face a mask of pure terror every time she managed to break the surface again. The current was dragging her quickly downstream while, on a rowboat, a man struggled with a woman.

"Brother David!" Tuck roared, but the man in the boat either didn't hear the friar or simply ignored him. There was a slapping sound as the shaven-headed Disciple landed a blow on Margaret's face, but the woman was gripping onto his sleeves for dear life, kicking and screaming and spitting like a feral cat as she tried to stop him from throwing her overboard along with her daughter.

There was a second great splash and Tuck looked around to see Scarlet powering through the water towards Denise, whose struggles had stopped by now and she'd begun to sink out of sight. The scene reminded Tuck horribly of the time when he'd been shot by an enemy crossbowman and ended up in a river himself. Like the girl, Tuck couldn't swim, and it had only been by the grace of God that the current had brought him ashore, unconscious and close to dying. The memory of those events crowded in upon the friar at that moment and he froze, feeling dread and terror taking a hold of him.

"Get in the water, you stupid bitch!" Brother David had lost patience now, as his boat was rocking unsteadily from side to side and there was every chance it would capsize and throw him into the Aire along with Margaret, who still refused to let him go, blind with rage as she was at the sight of her beloved girl sinking beneath the cold, black water. The sound of a fist hitting flesh carried horribly across the river then, as the Disciple hit Margaret again, and she fell back into the shallow hull. David touched a hand to his face, then looked at the blood there. The woman had managed to scratch him badly. "Right," he shouted in anger. "I'm done playing with you."

Margaret was lying senseless, unable to offer any more resistance, as Brother David bent and grasped her by the arm, and then the leg. It didn't take much effort for him to roll her limp body up, but, just as she was about to tip over into the water, there was a terrific snapping sound at Tuck's side, and the friar flinched instinctively, turning to see Little John, longbow in hand.

The bailiff was already fitting a second arrow to his string, but the first missile streaked through the air and hammered into Brother David's shoulder with terrific force. Before the Disciple could even cry out, he was thrown sideways, into the river.

"Wake up, Tuck," John commanded, dropping his bow and shaking off his boots and cloak. "Help Will – the current's too strong for him."

"Where are you going?" The friar asked, embarrassed at his lack of action as his two friends attempted to rescue the women.

"To get the boat before it drifts downstream," John replied, then dived into the river with an almighty splash.

Tuck ran to the water's edge, relieved to see Scarlet swimming towards him, face twisted in concentration. He had one arm around the girl and used his free hand to draw himself through the river towards the shore. It was slow work, for Scarlet was not the most experienced of swimmers and the current there was strong, so he was putting all his energy into reaching safety as quickly as possible, before some hidden danger, like a submerged log or reeds, snagged him or the unmoving girl.

Tuck looked down and was glad to see the water wasn't deep here at the edge. It had been, where Scarlet jumped in, but the current had pulled them a fair distance downstream and, thank God, this section was shallower. The friar shrugged off his cloak and grey cassock, tossing them onto the bank, and ran out into the freezing water. Although the river was shallow here at the edge, it quickly dropped off and he found himself with the water up to his chest. He felt panic rising in him again for deep water was one of the very few things in this world that frightened him, but Will reached out for him and they locked hands. Tuck used every ounce of strength in him to pull his friend and his silent burden forward, as he began moving backwards himself, fighting with every step to make sure the current didn't send him off balance.

At last, Scarlet's feet touched the bottom and, with Tuck's help, they carried the limp child out of the water, placing her onto the shore before they climbed up themselves. Scarlet immediately dropped to his hands and knees, while the friar rolled Denise onto her side. Water trickled out of her mouth and Tuck once again felt despair rising within him. He could not remember his own near-death drowning experience consciously, but, somehow, all of this seemed familiar. The thought of the girl dying before him seemed unbearable.

"Is she breathing?" Scarlet gasped. "If she's not breathing, roll her onto her back and press on her chest."

Tuck stared at Denise and it felt as though he himself was drowning but, as he watched, joy and relief flooded through him and he cried, "She's all right, Will! She's breathing!"

"Thank God," Scarlet mumbled, collapsing onto his back.

The sound of his teeth chattering finally brought Tuck back to his usual calm, confident self, and he grabbed his cassock from where he'd dropped it, threw it over his head, and then he hurried over to Will.

"Get your wet clothes off, Scarlet, quickly." He helped his friend strip then ran to his horse and took out the rolled-up blanket that was attached to the saddle. "Here, wrap this around yourself," he ordered, tossing it to the now naked Scarlet, who took it gratefully, covering his blotchy, purple-white skin with it and curling up to retain as much heat as possible.

"You'll have to do the same for the girl," Scarlet said in a gasping voice.

Tuck did not like the idea of stripping Denise but he knew that, if he didn't get her warm, she would surely die from the cold and shock of her experience. Still, he hesitated, glancing over his shoulder to see, with great relief, John rowing the boat towards them. It floated onto the shore and the bailiff helped Margaret out, watching as she sprinted past him and, gasping and sobbing, dragged herself up the little bank and dropped down, cradling her daughter's head in her hands.

"Take her clothes off, please," Tuck said, then repeated himself more forcefully as Margaret didn't take in his words the first time. At last she took his meaning and quickly started to remove her daughter's sodden garments while the friar once again ran for the horses, this time collecting the blankets from both Scarlet and John's animals. He returned to Margaret and gave her one of them, quickly turning away as the anguished mother wrapped it around her daughter and hugged her tightly, rubbing the blue, freezing limbs through the material, desperately trying to bring life back to them.

Tuck went now to Little John who'd just stepped up onto the bank and was walking, trudging, towards them with the air of one who'd just fought a great battle.

"Get that stuff off," the friar said, and John stared at him for a moment before he turned to look down at the shore of the Aire at his discarded, and still dry, cloak. "I'll get that," Tuck told him, you just get your wet things off before you freeze."

A short time later John was bundled up in both his own cloak and Tuck's, Scarlet was walking around in his blanket, stamping his feet and rubbing his arms, while Denise, with two blankets around her now, had regained consciousness. The girl and her mother held one another close and cried.

Tuck bustled about, finding thin, dry twigs and larger branches, before using the flint and steel he carried to start a fire next to the sodden girl and his two friends.

For a while no-one said anything. The only sounds were Denise and Margaret softly crying, until Scarlet said to John in a hollow voice, "What happened to David?"

"No idea," the bailiff replied. "I lost sight of him when I jumped into the water. Tuck? You see where he went?"

Friar Tuck shook his head. "No, I was looking at Will and Denise. I don't think he'll give us much trouble any more though. Assuming he made it out of the water, and gets your arrow out of his shoulder, he knows we're onto him. He'll ride as far and fast as he can away from Yorkshire in case we catch him."

"I wouldn't be so sure of that," Scarlet growled, staring at the opposite side of the riverbank. "Look."

There, just across from the little island the boat had been beside when the three companions arrived, was Lady Alice de Staynton, wrapping a blanket of her own around the tall figure of Brother David, before helping him onto the back of a horse. She slapped its rump, sending it trotting across the grass, before she mounted a second beast and followed David. She looked across the water at them but remained silent as she stared malevolently at each in turn and then, at last, they rode out of sight behind a grove of trees.

"What are you waiting for?" Scarlet demanded, snapping Tuck's head around in attention. "Get after them."

"He's right," John said. "She'll head for St Joseph's to gather her wealth and legal documents before they ride off to God-knows-where. We need to catch them before they escape, Tuck."

"I'm in no state for another chase," Scarlet said sorrowfully, and his bruised face and still-purpled skin lent weight to his words. "Someone will have to wait here and take care of ladies anyway, so it might as well be me."

Margaret shook her head and managed a weak smile at his words. "You're in no state to protect us either, Brother William. But you have my thanks for saving Denise, so I'll look after you until you're strong enough to ride home again."

"That's settled then," Scarlet said. "There's wine in my saddlebag, Margaret. We could all do with a drop, eh? And there's food too if you or Denise are hungry." He looked up at Tuck and John. "Are you two still here? Get your arses to the church then, go on!"

Friar and bailiff quickly followed his command and were soon racing along the track in the direction of St Joseph's, Scarlet's final, shouted words still ringing in their ears: "Don't let them escape. Not after all the work we've put in to bring them down!"

CHAPTER TWENTY-TWO

Little John was apprehensive about what they'd find at St Joseph's, shaking his head and muttering to himself the closer they got to the old church. Tuck, on the other hand, was still shamed by the fact he'd been no help whatsoever at the river and, as a result, was ready to make up for it by capturing Brother David. If that meant a fight, so much the better.

Tuck might be a man of God, but he would always be a warrior at heart.

"We're not going to get there before them," John called across to his friend as they thundered back along the westward track. "What are we going to do if Lady Alice tells the rest of her Disciples to stop us from arresting her?"

That wasn't a scenario Tuck had envisioned, and his desire for a battle cooled somewhat. They still had a job to do though, even if it meant going up against innocent men and women. "You have your staff," he shouted in return. "And I have my cudgel. The Disciples are, mostly, not going to be a threat if it comes to a fight, not against the pair of us. We'll just have to try not to hurt them too much."

John didn't reply but the friar had merely said what he'd been thinking anyway. Brother David had tried to murder a mother and her daughter, undoubtedly by the command of his Holy Mother – the bailiff had to arrest them for that crime, never mind all the others they would be accused of once they were in the hands of the law. If anyone stood in their way, they would simply have to be swept aside with as little bloodshed as possible.

The snow had started to fall again and, at the first village they passed, John slowed and called to a pair of young men who were feeding snorting hogs.

"You lads, come here!"

At the sound of his bellowing voice a middle-aged woman emerged from the house adjoining the pigpen, staring up at the riders suspiciously.

"There was a boating accident on the river," John told the villagers, pointing back along the road. "Two women and a man. They need dry clothes, food and, if possible, a ride on your wagon to someplace they can shelter and get their strength back." He fished out some coins, noting the woman's widening eyes as she took in their value, and tossed them to her. "I have more of those for you if you make sure our friends are safe."

One of the young men was already hurrying off, to find a horse or ox that could pull the wagon John had mentioned, while the other had disappeared into the house calling, "I'll gather bread and ale, Ma!"

Satisfied that Will and the women would be safely brought home before the snow proved a danger, John waved in salute to the woman, and then he and Tuck began riding hard once more for St Joseph's.

"Maybe we should stop in Altofts as well," the friar suggested when they were not far from their destination. "Gather some men to help us. It could save any bloodshed."

"No time," John shouted, shaking his head. "The longer it takes us to reach the church, the more chance they'll escape, and we'll never see them again."

Tuck was content to follow the bailiff's decision, for Little John had been Robin Hood's trusted second-in-command during their outlaw days and proven his wisdom on many occasions over the years.

The building appeared on the horizon at last, its dark stone walls and recently repaired roof standing out starkly against the white, frosty landscape.

"Remember, Tuck—we're here as representatives of the sheriff," John said as they brought their horses to a walk. "On official business, so no-one should be standing in our way."

"The sheriff? Never mind him," the friar replied, reining in his mount and climbing down from the saddle. "I'm here as a man of God, to put an end to this so-called 'Holy Mother' and her abomination of a sect. Woe betide any who try to stop me."

John joined his friend and hefted his quarterstaff as they stared at the closed doors of St Joseph's, wondering whether they should simply storm inside and hope for the best.

That decision was taken out of their hands as the doors suddenly burst open and Lady Alice de Staynton herself came hurrying out, a heavy sack over her shoulder and another in her hand. She spotted the bailiff immediately and muttered an exasperated curse before glancing back and calling, "David! Draw your sword. Disciples—gather your weapons, my children, for the representatives of the Black Lords have come to drag us all to hell."

"Oh, shit," John muttered as a great cry of outrage came from the gloomy interior of the church and a dozen or more men and women charged outside carrying whatever weapons they could muster. Brother David was right in the centre and he had a longsword in his hand. He carried it expertly, and there was no trace of fear on his face as he sized up his two enemies, only irritation.

Tuck strode forward, cudgel in hand and righteous fury in his eyes as he raised his arms and glared at the Disciples. "If you are truly men and women of God, you will stand aside and let us pass. Your leader" – he pointed at Lady Alice who was hurriedly trying to attach her sacks to her horse's saddle – "has been lying to you, as your own Brother, Colwin, will undoubtedly tell you himself."

"Where the hell is he?" John muttered behind him, for there was no sign of the young acolyte. Perhaps he'd already taken himself off, to live somewhere else, since he'd found out everything and everyone he believed in was a sham. "The one person that might have helped us and, for once, there's no sign of him. Typical."

The other shaven-headed, soldierly Disciple of God was there, though, and Brother David clearly had no intention of allowing Tuck or the bailiff to state their case. He raised his sword aloft and shouted, "They are the servants of Satan," he cried. "For months, years, we have fought the Black Lords without being able to see them with our Earthly eyes. Now, they grow bold enough to show themselves here, on consecrated, holy ground!"

One of the acolytes charged forward then, an expression of hatred on his face. He held a dagger which was designed for cutting meat at the dinner table but would most assuredly work perfectly adequately as a weapon against these 'real', flesh and blood Black Lords.

He came rushing towards them but, as soon as he was within range, John's staff swept out, clattering into the man's legs, sending him sprawling with a pained cry that cut off abruptly as the butt of the bailiff's weapon cracked against the back of his head.

"We're not Black Lords," Tuck shouted. "I am Friar Tuck, and this is Little John. You've surely heard of us. We're mortal men, and here to arrest this...'Holy Mother'... for killing your own brothers and sisters. At her command, Brother David just tried to drown Margaret and her daughter Denise on the River Aire—"

David ran forward himself then, knowing he had to bolster the other Disciples into an attack now, before the seeds of doubt could be sown in their minds. He ran for Tuck and aimed a savage cut at the portly friar, but Little John's massive staff snaked out and parried the sword with a clatter that rang through the snow covered churchyard.

"Come on," David shouted, half turning to exhort his fellow Disciples into action. They did move forward now, as one, but many of them had been confused by the friar's words. Why would he lie about this? And where *were* Margaret and Denise. They looked to Lady Alice for reassurance, but she was struggling to get her sacks tied to her horse for they were heavy and her fingers were numb from the cold, making it difficult to form a knot.

The size and commanding physical presence of Tuck, and Little John in particular, also made the

Disciples think twice about launching an attack on the frosty ground. Someone obviously felt it safer to strike a blow from afar, and a small rock careered through the falling snow, striking John in the face.

He saw the missile approaching a split-second before it struck him but, even so, he couldn't help reeling back in pain for it felt like his nose had been broken and he could already taste blood.

David saw an opening – he didn't fear Tuck for the friar's cudgel was surely too short to be much defence against his own longsword – and he stepped nimbly forward, but had to duck as another stone whistled past his ear. This one too struck John, this time flush on the forehead, and the giant bailiff roared with rage, but his vision swam, and he dropped to one knee, cursing loudly.

Tuck dropped his own short weapon which had served him so well over the years, and lifted John's quarterstaff, just in time to fend off Brother David who was advancing again. This time the friar went on the attack himself, throwing a flurry of swipes and thrusts, but the Disciple was well trained with a blade and managed to deflect each of Tuck's attacks.

"In the name of Christ and all His saints," the friar cried breathlessly, "stop this madness. There are no Black Lords and never were. You'll all be hanged if the bailiff dies from those injuries!"

"His mouth is the gate to hell, like all priests," Lady Alice called in a calm but firm voice and Tuck looked across to see her now mounted on her horse, gazing stonily back at him. "Kill them both, and send them back to their diabolical master, Satan."

Although the Disciples had battled imaginary, invisible demons, not all of them were convinced by their Holy Mother's words. Tuck and the massive bailiff, who was bleeding quite heavily, certainly *looked* like men. Confusion was plainly written on at least half of their faces, but, unfortunately for Tuck and John, others accepted Lady Alice's command without question and they stepped forward again now, weapons raised.

Little John struggled to his feet and, realising his quarterstaff was gone, drew his sword. He was unsteady but the sight of his bloody, bearded face and the naked steel in his hand caused the more timid of the Disciples to whimper. This was not how they'd envisioned life in the community.

Their day was only about to become even more confusing.

Another bruised and bloody figure appeared, this time from within St Joseph's itself. One of the Disciples near the doors noticed him and cried out at the sight of him.

"Brother Colwin, what happened to you?"

As the rest of the group looked around to see what was happening now, David once again attacked John, their blades coming together with terrible force, causing the bailiff to groan and stagger back as a wave of nausea coursed through him. The shaven-headed attacker didn't hesitate this time, thrusting the tip of his sword out and into John.

Tuck roared at the sight of the crimson blade and stepped forward, aiming his staff at David's head, but the man was too fast and easily knocked the wooden weapon to the side, then, with astonishing speed, kicked the friar hard between the legs.

"I told you these Black Lords could not stand against us, my Disciples!" Lady Alice cried out in triumph, as David loomed over Tuck, grinning savagely. "Finish it!"

The point of the sword tore straight through flesh and bone, exploding in a spray of blood from the front of Brother David's chest and everything fell silent. Tuck looked on, oblivious to the gore on his face as the shaven-headed Disciple of God fell forward onto the frozen ground. Behind him stood Brother Colwin, sword in hand, jaw clenched as he watched his one-time friend's body being slowly covered in soft, white snowflakes.

"What are you doing, Brother?"

"Oh, God above, help us, they've all gone mad!"

The Disciples were utterly bereft, either crying and screaming in horror at the terrible violence before them, or standing in silence as tears rolled down their cheeks.

Friar Tuck stood up, watching Brother Colwin warily, fearing the wronged acolyte may still turn on them in his madness, but the young Disciple was not interested. Instead, Colwin thrust his sword into the ground, the blood running slowly down the blade and forming a crimson patch in the pristine, white snow, and then he turned and started running towards Lady Alice, roaring like some enraged beast.

"Yah!" The Holy Mother screamed in fright and kicked her heels into her horse's flanks, thrusting it forward into a gallop that the man could not hope to match although that didn't stop him trying. The horse sped away along the eastern road, Colwin running in terrible, murderous silence at its back, arms and legs pumping rhythmically, until they were swallowed up by the worsening blizzard.

"I should go after them," Tuck muttered, but he had no appetite for the chase, not when his friend was bleeding and in danger of freezing to death. "Damn her," he decided, making his mind up and instantly becoming the self-assured, commanding friar of old. "You!" he roared, pointing at one of the younger male Disciples. "And you! Help the bailiff into the church, hurry, and be careful with him, by God! You there, you can fetch some clean water and bandages from wherever you people keep them and bring them to me. The rest of you," he glared imperiously at the cowed men and women who, with the departure of their leaders, were now much more pliable. "Get inside, put some more logs on the fire, and warm some ale for us all. This snow is only going to get worse."

"What about Brother David?" a terrified looking woman asked. "We can't just leave him there."

Tuck patted her shoulder reassuringly as he passed, oblivious to the blood coating his face. "He'll still be there when the snow stops falling, lady, and you can give him a proper burial. Come inside and warm yourself, it's been a shocking day for us all."

She began to sob and clutched at his cassock as he led her into the church and someone pushed the doors shut behind them, banishing the wind and the snow that had already half-covered Brother David's lifeless body.

CHAPTER TWENTY-THREE

Tuck was helped by two of the Disciples to bathe and bind Little John's injuries which, praise be to God, were not as bad as they'd seemed. Brother David's sword had made a deep wound in the bailiff's shoulder, and it would take a long time to heal, but Tuck was not too worried about that now that they'd cleaned it.

"It's those knocks to the head that you took," he said to the giant when he regained consciousness. "They could be dangerous and there's not a thing we can do about it. We'll just have to keep an eye on you for the next couple of days. If you feel sick or dizzy, let someone know straight away, all right?"

"Aye. Stop fussing will you," John grumbled, somewhat embarrassed to be lying, half-naked, within St Joseph's while the remaining Disciples of God stared at him in fear, wondering what would become of them now that their leader had abandoned them. "And clean that blood off your face, man, you look like a demon."

"Will we be arrested?" an elderly man, who Tuck guessed immediately must be Stephen Drinkwater, asked the bailiff when he was sitting with his back against the wall and a cup of warm ale in his hand.

"I shouldn't think so," John replied gloomily. "None of you knew what your Holy Mother was really up to, did you?" He stared around at the faces of those watching him but saw only concern and sadness, no duplicity. That was hardly proof of their innocence of course, but, right now, the last thing he wanted to do was alarm any of them, considering he and Tuck were effectively at their mercy.

"Only Lady Alice and Brother David should have faced justice," Tuck said with a small smile, touching Drinkwater on the arm before accepting a damp cloth from one of the other Disciples and wiping away as much of the blood on his face as he could. "Once the snow passes, me and the bailiff will be on our way and you can continue with your lives, I would expect. Margaret and Denise are safe, and they'll rejoin you soon enough."

"What about the Holy Mother?" someone said, in the tone of a nervous child, and Tuck wondered just how these acolytes would fare without their charismatic leader.

"I don't know," he replied, just as the doors opened and a gust of icy wind swept through the church.

All eyes turned to the threshold and there were gasps and mutters of horror and surprise as the red-faced, shaven-headed figure of Brother Colwin stomped inside, carrying the limp form of Lady Alice de Stayton over his shoulder.

"He's killed her! Oh, God, he's killed her too!"

Friar Tuck ignored the hysterical cries and walked towards the young man, surprised to see either him or the Lady again. "Is she…?"

"Not yet," Colwin said. "But she's freezing so you'd better get her warmed up or she'll not survive the night. Her horse slipped on a patch of ice and threw her. She's been like this ever since."

The friar reached out and lifted the unmoving Holy Mother from him and then carried her across to the fire. Someone pushed a bedroll over for him to place her on, and he asked the Disciples to take care of her. He had no idea which of them would be best suited to the task, and he had no inclination to find out, so he left them to work it out amongst themselves as he went back to Brother Colwin who hadn't moved from where Tuck left him.

They stared at one another for a moment, before the friar gently took him by the arm and guided him over to the hearth. "You're freezing too," he said gently, noting the young man's blue pallor and chattering teeth. "Sit there and warm yourself, while I fetch you a—Oh, thank you."

Stephen Drinkwater had already taken the hot poker from the burning logs and placed it into a cup of ale, which he handed to Brother Colwin now. It was accepted without a word and Tuck suspected the eventful day had all been too much for the young Disciple.

Outside, the wind had picked up and it howled around the church, almost as if God himself was berating the inhabitants for what had happened there, but they were warm and safe inside and Friar Tuck was a calming presence as he moved amongst them, smiling and offering blessings upon them.

Lady Alice eventually returned to consciousness and John ordered that she be given food and drink. This was consumed in silence, the Holy Mother eating with apparent calm dignity until, once she was finished, she looked at the bailiff and said, "Why have you come here, to our home, and caused all this trouble?"

John and Tuck shared a look—they knew they had to speak carefully here, or face turning the Disciples against them again. They never had to say anything, however, for Brother Colwin spoke up.

"You and Brother David have been lying to us all this time," he growled, walking across to stand over the woman who gazed back defiantly, apparently unworried by his accusation. "You lied to your own husband, Henry, and then commanded David to hire scum – outlaws probably – to attack your next husband, Elias, and burn down his house."

"What absolute nonsense," Lady Alice retorted, looking around at the silent Disciples. "You all know me better than that. Don't believe these lies." Then she turned to Little John, and her lip curled ever so slightly in a smile. "Can you prove a single one of the accusations against me?"

"That's not my job," the bailiff replied. "That's for cleverer men than me to do. But" – now he too addressed the Disciples – "what your Brother says is true. The Holy Mother stands accused of the crimes he mentioned, but also of ordering the murders of your Sister Margaret and her daughter."

Stephen Drinkwater's face had turned pale as he listened, but he shook his head now. "These are terrible crimes you accuse her of. I can hardly take it all in. It seems unbelievable!"

"Be that as it may," John replied firmly. "I personally saw Brother David trying to throw Margaret into the river. The only reason he didn't manage it was because, as you might have noticed, I hit him in the shoulder with an arrow."

Indeed, the Disciples had wondered what had happened to David's arm when he returned to the church with Lady Alice that afternoon, so the bailiff's story made sense to them. But Brother Colwin wasn't finished.

"Apart from all that," he said. "Our Holy Mother, who taught us all the virtues of a chaste life, was enjoying the pleasures of the flesh in that Godforsaken bedchamber right there." He pointed in the direction of the Lady's room. "With Brother David!"

For some strange reason, this accusation brought cries of outrage from the acolytes. It was as if murder was a minor transgression compared to the heinous sin of sexual congress. John looked at Tuck in amazement, but his confusion didn't matter. All that mattered was the fact that Brother Colwin's charge had finally turned the Disciples, for now at least, against their Holy Mother.

Lady Alice's face was scarlet with rage and shame and she rounded on Colwin. "You're just jealous, *boy*. I knew you wanted me for yourself – this is just your way of getting back at me for not allowing you into my bed."

"But you took Brother David into it readily enough," Tuck said coolly.

"David was my companion for years," she said, sorrow now tempering her rage as she thought of the acolyte dead in the whirling snow outside. "He was the bastard son of a nobleman, unloved by his family and despised by the people in his town who'd been ill-treated by his cruel father. When we met, it became instantly clear that we should do God's work together. Of course, we became close. Other Disciples came and went over the years, but David always stayed faithfully by my side." She turned her attention back to Colwin, sneer once more on her round face. "You took it upon yourself to act like the great protector of us all, taking Brother David's quiet nature for a weakness, or a need to be led. Little did you know he thought you a fool, and laughed at you when your back was turned. He was all man, while you are nothing but a boy."

Tuck could see the Lady's bitter words hammering home like arrows in Brother Colwin and decided they'd all heard enough. He hurried across and pulled the Holy Mother to her feet before guiding her through the vestry and along the corridor to her bedchamber where he locked her inside. The windows were too small to fit through, even if she could reach them and smash her way out, and there were no other exits. She screamed at this imprisonment and, from the sounds of it, began smashing what meagre furniture was in the room, but no-one paid her any heed and, at last, all became silent apart from the wind blowing outside.

It was not the most comfortable evening for the men from Wakefield, since John wouldn't be much use in a fight should the confused Disciples decide to attack them, and Tuck dreaded the thought of hurting the acolytes. As it turned out, however, the unexpected return of Brother Colwin seemed to offer the others some reassurance in such bewildering times. They knew him as a good, honest man, who had protected them in the past, and his actions that day had said enough.

As had Lady Alice de Staynton's.

The snow, and John's injuries, meant night closed in with them all trapped inside St Joseph's. John slept while Tuck remained awake and alert, and they swapped places midway through the night, but there was no trouble and, when dawn broke, they made ready to leave. The Disciples were sombre and quiet, but Brother Colwin seemed to have regained some of his composure with the rising sun. He ordered food and drink be packed for Tuck and John, just in case their relatively short journey to Pontefract—where they would hand Lady Alice over to the castle steward for later trial—was interrupted by another blizzard.

"Are you sure you're in a fit state to make this journey?" Tuck asked John as they made ready to leave. In truth, the giant bailiff appeared quite over the previous day's assaults but it was still cold and the friar worried for his wounded friend.

"Well, you can't take the Lady to Pontefract yourself," came the firm reply. "I'm feeling fine now anyway. Shoulder is aching like hell, but I've had worse and survived. We'll get her to the castle, then ride home to Wakefield as soon as possible and Amber can take care of me." He grinned at the thought, as did Tuck, and together they walked along the chilly corridor behind Brother Colwin to get Lady Alice from her chamber.

She flew for Colwin as soon as the door opened, attempting to rake his face and eyes with her nails, but he easily overpowered her and the bailiff tied her hands together with rope the Disciples used to dry their laundered clothes on.

"Now, keep your fists to yourself," he told her. "Or I'll tie your legs as well, and throw you over the back of my horse to ride into Pontefract like a sack of cabbages."

She spat at him, but she was so small the spittle barely reached his chest, much less his face, which she'd been aiming for. John merely shook his head in disgust and they marched her outside, helping her up onto the friar's saddle before Tuck mounted the horse behind her, and John clambered onto his own mare.

"Where did you find her last night?" the bailiff asked Brother Colwin. "I'd like to catch her horse if I can. No doubt she had some incriminating documents in its saddlebags, not to mention coins that would, surely, belong to your group."

Colwin pointed along the road in the direction they would be travelling towards Pontefract and described the tree he'd discovered Lady Alice beneath. Then he met John's gaze and said, "Are you really just riding away and leaving us to be about our lives here?"

"Well, it's not up to me," John said. "But I don't see any reason why there should be trouble for your sect now that we've got the Lady in custody. There's been no suggestion anyone other than Brother David was involved in her crimes and…" He glanced at the spot where the dead Disciple's body had lain the previous day. It had been moved by Stephen Drinkwater and some of the other acolytes, leaving only some muddy footprints and red stain in the snow. "And you, personally, saved our lives, Brother," the bailiff admitted with a nod. "Rather than being in any trouble, I think you should be in for a reward."

The rest of the Disciples came to watch them leave, and a woman called out in a soft, meek voice. "What will become of us though? I mean, we have no-one to lead us anymore."

"She's right," another man said, and he seemed so lost and upset by everything that had happened that he practically hid behind his fellows. "We need someone to take care of us—that's why we're here in the first place!"

John frowned, and opened his mouth as if he was about to tell the people to grow up and behave like adults rather than children, but Tuck broke in, his calm but strong voice drawing every eye to him.

"I don't think there's any problem. Brother Colwin may be young, but that's not a bad thing. He can lead you."

The shaven-headed Disciple stared at him, but Stephen Drinkwater stepped forward to stand beside him, nodding his bald head. "I think that's a good solution to our problem," the old man said, and some of the others muttered agreement, smiling with obvious relief that they wouldn't be left to fend for themselves.

Tuck looked at Brother Colwin and, had they been alone, he would have apologised for throwing the young man into this situation when he was trying to come to terms with everything himself. But they all needed Colwin to be strong for now, despite his youth. He was truly the only one of the Disciples who could be counted on to organise them and make sure they got through the coming days and weeks.

There were no arguments for Will Scarlet came cantering along the road towards them at that moment. When he reached them, he grinned at John and Tuck, overjoyed to see them alive and with Lady

Alice safely in custody. He managed a curt nod at Brother Colwin, who returned the gesture, and then the smile appeared on Scarlet's face again as he held up two sacks.

"Look what I found," he said. "There was a dead horse on the road, must have broken it's leg then froze to death in the snow, poor beast. I recognised it as the Holy Mother's and found these attached to the saddle."

Lady Alice stared murderously at him, but she knew there was no point saying anything so remained silent.

"Keep a hold of them for now," Little John said. "We'll take them to Pontefract to be used as evidence against the woman. Rest assured, though" – he spoke to Brother Colwin again – "any money that's in there will be returned to you, since I believe I'm correct in saying individual Disciples can't own wealth or property? So, whatever belonged to Lady Alice, belonged to your sect as a whole."

Tuck grinned. "That's perfectly correct, John."

"You're fools," the Holy Mother said to them, however, her tone dripping with venom. "I've done nothing wrong, and you'll never prove that I have. It was all Brother David."

John pursed his lips and shrugged, wincing as his wound flared painfully. "You might be right. We'll see."

They left for Pontefract then, John, Tuck, and Will Scarlet, with their prisoner. The Disciples of God watched them go, bereft and stunned by the loss of their leader, but relieved and hopeful for the future now that Brother Colwin was going to look after them.

Maybe their war against the Black Lords had finally been won.

CHAPTER TWENTY-FOUR

"I'm sorry, John, but that's just the way it is. There's nothing I can do."

The bailiff shook his head, sighing in disgust at Sir Henry de Faucumberg's words. Once, the Sheriff of Nottingham and Yorkshire had been an enemy to John and his friends in Robin Hood's outlaw band, but now he was John's employer and they had become quite friendly over the years. Even so, the nobleman was firm in his refusal to do anything about Lady Alice de Staynton.

"You must be able to do something, my lord," John muttered. "You're the sheriff, for God's sake."

"She simply hasn't broken any laws," de Faucumberg replied, spreading his hands wide and placing his booted feet on the sturdy table that separated him from John, Friar Tuck and Will Scaflock. "Well, I'm quite sure she *has*, in fact, broken quite a few laws, but there's nothing we can actually prove."

"What about the man I've got imprisoned in Altofts?" John said. "Clibert? He'll testify against the woman. He told me himself that he pretended to be a barber-surgeon so that Henry of Castellford would take his own life."

The sheriff bobbed his head. "Oh yes. And what law would that be breaking, exactly?"

John frowned, but had no reply to the question.

"I'll tell you," the sheriff growled. "None. It's not a crime to pretend to be a damn barber-surgeon, John."

"But it pushed the man over the edge," Scarlet cried in exasperation. "And what about them pushing the two women in the river to drown them? We saw that with our own eyes." He folded his arms across his chest, but the sheriff shook his head.

"You saw Lady Alice pushing someone into the river, did you? No, of course not, the woman is far too clever to be caught out like that." He stood up and paced back and forward behind his desk. "You saw the man – Brother David was it? Yes, you saw him trying to drown the women. And he's already faced justice, hasn't he? He was killed, so we can't ask him to testify against the Lady! Both the women survived anyway." Although he could not take any action against the Holy Mother it was clear Sir Henry de Faucumberg was as angry about it as the three former outlaws.

"So, you're just going to let her walk out of Pontefract Castle?" Tuck said in a neutral voice, although the sheriff's eyes blazed angrily.

"You know as well as I do, Brother Tuck, how the law works. Without proof of wrongdoing, there's nothing to be done." He waved his hand vaguely in the air. "Oh, perhaps we could look through her accounts and find something to find her guilty of, but it wouldn't be enough to do anything other than fine her. And I don't think Sir Henry of Grosmont would be happy if we left her in his castle at Pontefract any longer without some charge."

The men looked at one another dejectedly. To have put in so much effort for nothing...It was a bitter draught to swallow.

"What the hell do we do then?" Scarlet asked. "She'll walk out of there and go straight back to St Joseph's. I've spent a lot of time with the Disciples of God and I know what kind of power she has over them. It won't be long before she's got them under her spell again, and she'll simply carry on as before."

De Faucumberg sat down again, his nervous energy mostly spent although he continued to tap his fingers on the desk as he gazed at Will, Tuck and John in turn. "I have no idea," he admitted. "You could try and find some people in Yorkshire who've had bad dealings with the Disciples and get them to offer testimony against the Lady. Other than that…" He shrugged and left the sentence unfinished.

As the bailiff led his friends out of the room, the sheriff called out, "Take some time to rest, John, you've earned it. I'll have more work for you whenever you're ready. And don't take this to heart, boys. Sometimes the law is as much use as a sword made of butter. It punishes those it should not, and lets real criminals go free – as you all know only too well."

"Thank you, my lord," John replied, closing the door and wandering, shoulders slumped, along the corridor back towards the stables.

The three men did not talk all the way there. They found their horses had been fed, watered and rubbed down by the stable boys; handing the lads coins as a reward, they mounted up in silence. Not until they'd passed through the city's Carter Gate and were riding along the northern road did John say anything.

"What are we going to do about this?" he asked. "We can't just let her win."

Scarlet opened his mouth to begin an angry tirade about the law, but Tuck spoke first, and his fury was a surprise to both of his friends, for he had generally been the calm, wise figure amongst all of Robin Hood's old gang.

"You're damn right we can't let her win," the friar said vehemently. "She's made fools of her acolytes and abused the Church's teachings. The woman is a killer and…an abomination!"

"Aye," Scarlet agreed. "But what are we going to *do* about it?"

"If the law won't find her guilty of murder," Tuck replied grimly, "we'll have to find some authority that *will* convict her, of something just as serious."

John and Scarlet eyed one another in confusion, and the bailiff demanded, "Like what?"

"Heresy, of course," said Tuck in a low voice, and his face was ashen as he spoke the words, for he knew better than any of them what happened to heretics.

* * *

They rode directly to St Joseph's, where Brother Colwin came out to meet them, accompanied by Sister Margaret, who smiled warmly at Will and even hugged him once he'd dismounted. He looked a little uncomfortable at the show of affection, but he grinned and asked how Denise was doing after her near drowning just a few days earlier.

"She's doing very well," Margaret replied. "Thanks to you, Brother William."

"Just call me Will, or Scarlet," he said, a little sheepish over the fact he'd pretended to be someone he was not, in order to infiltrate their group. His actions in saving Denise's life meant Margaret held only affection for him though, and Colwin invited them all inside to warm themselves by the fire for their hands and faces were red from the cold.

It seemed Colwin and Margaret had naturally assumed the job of leading the Disciples of God through this tumultuous period in their history and Scarlet was pleased to see everyone in the church smiling and apparently somewhat at ease with life again, despite the loss of their beloved Holy Mother. Some worked with needle and thread to mend clothes, while others sat in a circle discussing a passage from the Bible, and Stephen Drinkwater whistled a hymn from halfway up a ladder as he wiped down the stained-glass windows.

"Your troubles aren't finished yet, I'm afraid," Little John said quietly to Colwin and Margaret as they all huddled around the hearth. The bailiff rubbed his frozen hands together, trying to bring some life back to them as he went on. "Lady Alice is to be set free. The sheriff says there's not enough evidence to prove she committed any crime serious enough to warrant the expense and trouble of a trial."

Margaret looked like she might cry at the news, but Brother Colwin did not appear surprised. He knew only too well how clever the Holy Mother was, and how she manipulated others to do her dirty work while keeping her own hands clean.

"She will come back here and convince our fellow Disciples that it was all a mistake, that she's innocent, and they will believe her, because they love her and want to believe she's infallible."

Little John nodded. "I believe you're probably right."

"I won't let her," Colwin hissed, and his hand fell to his sword, the one which he'd used to end Brother Colwin's life, retrieved from where he'd plunged it into the snow that fateful day.

"Don't be foolish," Friar Tuck admonished the young man. "It was all right for you to kill Colwin, for he was about to slaughter the bailiff and me. But killing Lady Alice would mean you'd be tried for murder, and you would hang for it, trust me." He stared at Colwin until the Disciple met his eyes. "Don't throw away your life for her. I have a better idea, and I will need your help."

Brother Colwin listened to the friar's plan, nodding periodically as he took it all in, and, when Tuck was finished, the Disciple agreed to play his part without hesitation. Sister Margaret was not so eager, however, and shrank away from the whole thing, which Tuck accepted. Despite everything that had happened, Margaret still loved the Holy Mother and, while she wanted to be free of her, Tuck's plan was a step too far for her.

"That's fine," Little John said reassuringly. "Brother Colwin's testimony, along with Scarlet's, should be enough."

Margaret looked ashamed but relieved, and excused herself, saying she had to take a warm drink to her daughter who was resting in the back bedchamber which had belonged to Lady Alice until recently. When she was gone, Tuck explained to Brother Colwin exactly what would be required of him for their plan to succeed. The Disciple's resolve never wavered for a moment—the revelation that his spiritual leader, along with his closest friend, Brother David, had betrayed everything they stood for, had turned Colwin utterly against them.

"Have no fears," he said to them as they headed through the doors towards their waiting horses once again. "I'll do what's needed to see her ruined, and my Brothers and Sisters free of her dark influence once and for all."

As the lawman and his friends rode off to put into motion the next part of their plan, Brother Colwin watched them go and stared at the small piece of ground where he'd plunged the point of his sword into David. It was the first time he'd killed a man but, as he stared out across the land and the road that led to Pontefract, he vowed to do the same to Lady Alice de Staynton if she turned up at the church and attempted to seize control of the Disciples once again, whether it meant he would hang or not.

CHAPTER TWENTY-FIVE

"Is it true that Lady Alice de Staynton said, 'the mouth of all priests is the gate to hell'?" Wulstan, the bishop leading the trial said to Brother Colwin. "Indeed, that she said this about our learned friend there: Robert Stafford?" He pointed towards the tonsured figure at the very front of the gathered audience. "More commonly known as Friar Tuck."

"That's right," Colwin replied in a firm, clear voice. "She said that just before she ordered us to kill the friar and the bailiff."

There were gasps of dismay from the onlookers at this revelation and the Bishop Wulstan's mouth twitched in the beginnings of a smile. This witness was proving as useful as Tuck had promised.

Rather than setting the Lady free, as the sheriff had suggested, she had simply been taken under guard from Pontefract Castle to All Saints Church right beside it, where she now faced these charges of heresy.

It had all been orchestrated by Friar Tuck, whose contacts in the Church proved most useful. The powerful bishop, Wulstan Branford—after losing his own diocese in Worcester a couple of years earlier—had been working as a helper to Archbishop Melton of York and staying in Pontefract at that time. Tuck had gone to see him and explained the situation, begging the bishop for his help in bringing Lady Alice before the ecclesiastical court. Bishop Wulstan had only met Tuck in person once before, but his old friend, Bishop Salmon of Norwich, had often told him the story of how the brave friar had saved his life when violent robbers waylaid him. So, when Tuck asked Bishop Wulstan for help, the influential clergyman had gladly agreed and set about organising the trial they were witnessing now.

"Is it also true," demanded Bishop Wulstan, "that Lady Alice, your so-called *Holy Mother*, would lead your sect in battles against invisible demons, before retiring to her room and allowing one of your number, a Brother Colwin, to use her body in strange and unnatural ways?"

Colwin's jaw tightened at the question, and Tuck wondered if he would deny this particular accusation, since he'd never actually seen the Lady and Colwin in bed together, merely hearing their exploits through the chamber door that one time, but the young acolyte nodded firmly. "Yes, that is true."

Again, there were gasps and murmurs of titillated outrage. Sex was always a good topic to get the people gossiping during a trial, Bishop Wulstan knew.

"What about this claim of hers?" the bishop said, reading from some notes on the parchment in his hand. "That she, the Lady Alice de Staynton," he nodded in the woman's direction and she glared at him in silent fury, "'resembled in every aspect, Mary, the Mother of God'?"

"She said that to our group on several occasions," Brother Colwin confirmed, and the people were angry now, for, as everyone knew, the Virgin Mary was like no other woman and had no successor on Earth. To claim otherwise was blasphemy on a terrible scale.

"What about your Holy Mother's late husband?" The bishop asked, checking his notes again. "Henry of...Castellford. He committed suicide, did he not? A mortal sin. Yet your people buried him within the grounds of St Joseph's, as they did with"– another pause to read the paper before him – "Brother Morris and" – Bishop Wulstan looked up and pulled a face clearly designed to be both amazed and comical – "Brother Elias—*another* husband of the Lady Alice!" A ripple of gasps and muted laugher ran around the gathering before the churchman continued in a harsher tone. "Were you aware that a man who takes his own life should not be buried in consecrated ground?"

Brother Colwin nodded. "Of course, your grace. But Lady Alice told us that Henry had not committed suicide—he had nobly chosen to leave this life so that he might carry on the fight against the Black Lords on their own plane of existence. It was not a cowardly act, or a sin. Quite the opposite, in fact, according to the Holy Mother."

Such a suggestion was so outlandish that it took many of the people gathered there a moment to take it in, and then, inevitably, most blessed themselves, muttering, "Father, son, and holy ghost," to ward off evil.

"And finally, what about this?" Bishop Wulstan demanded, lifting the simple wooden cross which he wore on a leather thong around his own neck. "What did your self-proclaimed 'Holy Mother' say about the cross?"

Colwin did not hesitate. "When we began living in St Joseph's, she made us take down all the crosses within the building and burn them." Men and women howled in fury at this ultimate sacrilege, and Colwin waited until their voices had dropped to an angry murmur before continuing. "She said the instrument on which Christ was tortured and killed was not to be venerated, for it was an evil symbol."

The bishop's eyes narrowed. He, of course, already knew about this accusation for it was in his own notes, but hearing it from this shaven-headed, intense young man, was shocking nonetheless. To decry the very symbol upon which the Catholic faith was built…It was incredible.

The people gathered within the room, from the lowest peasant to the church elders who presided over this trial, were talking amongst themselves, voices raised in righteous, vengeful anger, and Bishop Wulstan knew his job was done. Everyone was convinced that Lady Alice de Staynton was a heretic—there was no need to even ask whether she denied the charges for William Scaflock of Wakefield, a man well known and respected by the people of Yorkshire, had already given his testimony against the woman that morning. So too had Henry of Castellford's daughter, Elspeth, who stated that the Lady Alice had bewitched her father into marrying her, using weird magical powers, an accusation the bishop obviously believed.

Lady Alice's guilt was not in doubt.

All that remained was for the bishop to offer her the chance to renounce her previous deeds and heretical beliefs, and they could move on from there.

Brother Colwin was thanked for his truthfulness and dismissed. He nodded respectfully to the bishop and walked over, to take his place beside Tuck, Scarlet and Little John while guards brought Lady Alice down to face the court.

Standing before them, middle-aged, plump, and homely, it was hard for the audience to understand how this woman had come to enjoy a position of power over what, by all accounts, were decent, God-fearing people. Her face was set in a grim, blank expression, but those watching could tell by the fidgeting of her hands that she was frightened. And with good reason—although it wasn't common for heretics to be denounced in England, there had been a great many of them burned at the stake over the past two hundred or so years in Europe. Those tales were lurid and explicit and all who heard them shivered at the agonies the victims must have endured.

Would that be the fate of Lady Alice de Staynton?

Certainly, if she would not renounce her diabolical beliefs there would be no helping her.

Bishop Wulstan spoke to the Lady, asking her to confirm who she was, and reminding her of the charges against her. She merely stared at him, lip curled disdainfully, and then he asked if she would disavow her previous, heretical beliefs and return to the Church's loving bosom.

"What will happen to me if I do?" she asked, eyes boring into the bishop.

He didn't reply for a moment, merely looked at her, almost as if he were daydreaming, until one of the other churchmen hissed at him to answer and he came back to himself with a start. "Er…" flustered he had to think for a few seconds, to remember what her question had been, and then, with a suspicious look on his face, as if fearing she'd bewitched him, he said, "You will be given a place in St Clement's Priory in York, and live your life there in peace, as a valued member of God's true Church."

"A nunnery?" Lady Alice demanded. "So, you will take everything from me, and force me to live as a nun, locked away from the world?" She spat on the floor at the bishop's feet. "I spoke the truth when I said your tongues were the gates to hell. You and all these other arse-licking priests—"

The rest of her diatribe was lost in the babble of voices, as the gathered clergymen and onlookers erupted in horror. Some, particularly the peasants, appeared more amused than outraged, Tuck noticed, but that was unimportant. In fact, it would help the story of what had happened here spread faster and wider, for people always enjoyed a good laugh at a bishop's expense.

Someone at the back of the church shouted, "Guilty!" and within moments his cry had been taken up by others, until the whole, vast chamber was filled with the chant.

"Guilty! Guilty! Guilty! Heretic! Heretic! Heretic!"

Tuck could see Bishop Wulstan speaking to Lady Alice but he had to read his lips to understand what he was saying to her. Not that it mattered, for it was plainly obvious that she'd condemned herself by her own harsh, offensive words, and, sure enough, that's exactly what the bishop was telling her.

The guards closed in and grasped her by the arms. The Lady's face was ashen and Tuck felt a momentary pang, pitying the woman; until he thought of her crimes and the men and possibly women that had died thanks to her evil machinations, and his resolve hardened again.

The Lady was dragged outside, past the howling onlookers in the church but, if she hoped to find an escape from their twisted faces and angry voices she was soon disabused of the notion for there was an even bigger mob gathered outside in the winter sunshine. Word of what had happened at the trial within the church had already filtered out to them and the guards had to be joined by more of their comrades for the people would have attacked Lady Alice without the soldiers to hold them at bay.

"What will they do to her?" Little John asked Tuck, shouting to be heard as they shoved their way through the people striving to get outside.

"Burn her!" an old woman cried, cackling with glee before she was shouldered aside by some other peasant and disappeared back into the crowd.

Tuck merely shook his head. He did not know what punishment the bishop and his fellows would mete out to the Holy Mother and he wasn't sure he wanted to find out. Despite her heinous acts, the friar was not one to enjoy watching the suffering of others, even criminals.

The vast majority of those gathered around them did not share his feelings, of course. The cries of "Burn her!" rang out all across the city. It had been a while since there had been a good execution, and the street vendors had been preparing for this event for days.

Sister Margaret grasped Tuck by the arm, tears running down her cheeks. "They're not going to burn her, are they? Please, God, you can't let them!"

The friar looked down at her sadly. Lady Alice had to be punished for her crimes, and stopped from returning to St Joseph's to repeat them, but the thought of the woman being immolated thanks to his actions was not a pleasant one. He swallowed, feeling bitter bile in his throat, but he shook his head, and said, as if to convince himself as much as Margaret, "Normally, if they're going to burn someone, the heretic is forced to carry the faggots and throw them onto the fire themselves. I don't see anything like that, so…"

Margaret's head dropped and she clung to Tuck like a child holding onto a parent in the midst of a thunderstorm. "I don't want her to come back to us," she sobbed. "Not after everything she's done. But – burning is a horrible death. The other Disciples would never get over it. They love her still!"

Tuck was always amazed by the behaviour and emotions of his fellow men and women. Despite the fact Lady Alice de Staynton had ordered David to murder Margaret and her beloved daughter, the woman still felt a loyalty and affection for her disgraced Holy Mother. The contrast this compassion – misplaced, in Tuck's view – made with the gleeful calls of the mob to burn the prisoner at the stake was extraordinary.

Margaret's legs suddenly gave way and the friar instinctively grasped her in his arms as she fell. He realised she'd fainted and decided they'd seen enough.

"John!" he called, then, when the bailiff, who was tall enough to see over everyone else in the crowd, turned to him, he said, "It's too much for Sister

Margaret, and, honestly, I've no desire to watch this myself any more. I'll take her to the tavern by the gate, you know the one?"

Little John did know it, and he agreed to his friend's plan. "All right, Tuck," he said. "You be careful on your way there, though. You know what an angry mob can be like: they take liberties. We'll join you there once this is finished, and I'll bring your horse with me."

Tuck nodded and began to push his way through the people. He was strong, and Margaret wasn't a heavy burden, but he was thankful that a path opened for him once those gathered around him realised he had a sickly woman in his arms.

Soon enough, they left the noisy crowd behind and Margaret came back to herself. Tuck explained what had happened and then they walked in silence until they reached the tavern not far away from the western gate. There, he bought two mugs of strong ale and the pair sat in the shadows, trying not to think what horrors Lady Alice was suffering at the hands of the bishop and the howling, bloodthirsty rabble.

CHAPTER TWENTY-SIX

"Burn her!"

"Kill her!"

"Gouge her eyes out!"

Little John was disgusted by the cries from the mob as Lady Alice was taken onto the raised platform in the town centre and paraded before them by a pair of grim soldiers. Bishop Wulstan let the shouts ring out, let the crowd work itself into a frenzy, before he raised his hands wide as if he was in a pulpit and about to celebrate mass.

The clergyman began to speak but John, Will and Brother Colwin were too far away, and the rabble yet too noisy, for them to hear what was being said.

"Excommunication," Colwin said eventually, and his face was pale. That word, at least, was impossible to miss, as it became the new chant of the outraged citizens who took it up before howling in vicious glee at the sight of something even John, towering over everyone around them, couldn't quite make out.

"What is it?" Will demanded, trying fruitlessly to see through the tightly packed bodies before him. "What are they doing?"

"I don't know," the bailiff replied, before finishing with a lame, "Oh."

A hush fell across the city then, as another soldier climbed the steps up to the wooden platform with something in his hand. Something that glowed with a fiery red letter 'H' at its end.

Will knew exactly what was about to happen when he saw that implement, for he'd used one himself many times to burn his mark on the thick hides of the cattle that belonged to his small farm.

The Church were branding Lady Alice de Staynton, not with a mark of ownership, but with a letter that would let everyone know what she was: a heretic.

There was a scream, and John and Will were glad when it was drowned out by the wrathful cheering and laughing of the bloodthirsty crowd. Colwin stared ahead, showing no outward emotion, but his jaw was clenched and his eyes were wet with unshed tears.

"Maybe this was a mistake," Scarlet muttered, shaking his head in anguish at their part in this terrible spectacle. "This is all our doing. Maybe we should have just told her to leave Yorkshire and be on her way."

John sighed heavily but shook his head. "She'd just have moved on and killed other innocent men and women in her quest for riches, Will. You know it as well as I do. She had to be stopped – had to face justice. At least they're not burning her."

"Yes, they are!" Will retorted.

"You know what I mean. They've excommunicated her, and branded her, but they're not burning her to death at the stake."

Bishop Wulstan was speaking again, arms raised aloft as he stared skywards, weak sunshine bathing his face. "Now, we banish this lady from our town! Let none grant her aid or succour on pain of excommunication themselves." He nodded to the soldiers guarding the disgraced Holy Mother and they tore her tunic so her back was bare, then they made her walk down the steps and into the crowd.

Somehow, as if knowing in advance that this would happen, many of the folk gathered there had switches and willow wands in their hands already, and they used them now to flog Lady Alice towards the southern gate of the town. The guards had to be careful, for the blows were wild and aimed haphazardly.

"This is barbaric," Little John spat. "It's like a twisted repeat of Christ being beaten and jeered as he carried his cross towards Calvary."

"Who knows? Perhaps that's the point," Will muttered, his words swallowed by the howling of the mob who were moving away to the south now, following the Lady, and Bishop Wulstan who was mouthing prayers piously as he walked.

Will Scarlet did not follow them and neither did the bailiff or Brother Colwin. Their part in the Holy Mother's trial was, thankfully, over.

* * *

It felt like an age before Little John, Will Scarlet and Brother Colwin walked into the alehouse, although it could only have been an hour or two at most.

"Did they—" Sister Margaret's question ended in a choked sob, but the bailiff leaned down and gave her a hug.

"No, lass, they didn't burn her at the stake if that's what you're worried about."

"They didn't?" Tuck demanded for, although he'd suggested the lack of faggots meant there would be no fires that day, he'd not really believed it himself, it had just been a way for him calm down the distraught female Disciple.

"She's not dead then?" The initial relief in Margaret's voice had changed to trepidation, perhaps as she thought of Lady Alice already making her way back to St Joseph's to take up her mantle of Holy Mother once again. She looked fearfully at Colwin, who took a stool beside her and grasped her hand.

"Don't worry," he said, nodding his thanks as a serving girl placed a mug of ale before him and the other newcomers. "The Lady will not be coming back to haunt us—dead or alive, she's not our problem anymore."

Margaret stared at him, and then she mumbled, "You're lying, aren't you? So that I don't get upset. They did kill her, didn't they?"

"You can believe him," Scarlet said firmly. "I swear to you, Lady Alice de Staynton left the city on her own two feet today, alive. You can move on with your lives and forget all about her."

It seemed as though Sister Margaret might demand more of an explanation but, after a time she simply nodded and stared at the dregs of ale in her mug.

"What'll happen to the rest of us now?" Colwin asked Tuck. "Will we just be forgotten about and left in peace, like you said?"

The friar shook his head. "Not quite, but don't be fearful. Bishop Wulstan will visit you at St Joseph's and ask you all to renounce Lady Alice's teachings. You'll have to sign documents to that effect, and to confirm that you accept the Church's teachings."

"We'll do that gladly," Margaret said, and then, after a few moments, she said softly to Colwin, "Can we go back home now?"

Colwin smiled and got to his feet, tipping the last of his drink into his mouth. "Good idea, I always hated big towns. Let's go. The sooner we leave, the sooner we can put all this behind us and move forward with our brothers and sisters in St Joseph's."

Margaret thanked Tuck, John and Scarlet for everything and headed towards the door as Colwin bent to grasp the hands of the three former outlaws.

"Once the sheriff sorts out all the legal details," John told him, "he's promised to return to you the sack of money we seized from the Holy Mother. Perhaps you could use it to have a proper chimney built in St Joseph's instead of that smoke hole Clibert put in the roof…"

The shaven-headed young man, and unlikely new leader of the Disciples of God, gave a wry smile and said, "Will you men ride with us? We're all heading east, but it's a few hours journey and it's always safer to travel in numbers."

"Aye," John agreed. "Of course, my friend. You get going. We'll finish our drinks and then catch up with you on the road, all right?"

Colwin dipped his head in acquiescence and led Margaret out to his waiting horse. The sound of the animal's hoofs faded into the distance and then, ale mug in hand, Friar Tuck looked at his friends.

"All right, what really happened to Lady Alice?" he demanded. "I'm glad they didn't burn her alive, for that would be a heavy burden for me to bear, but there must be more to the tale than what you told Margaret."

Little John sighed and stared into his drink. "You're right," he said grimly, and told his friend everything that had taken place in the town centre. He shook his head in disgust once the tale was finished. "Like animals they were, Tuck. We've all seen this kind of thing before. It makes me sick to see men and women acting like savages, then going back about their daily lives as if nothing's happened."

They sipped their drinks quietly for a while, each wondering what would become of the branded woman. Without anyone to turn to for aid, and not even a tunic to keep the winter cold from her bare back, her life was going to be nothing more than a desperate fight for survival over the coming days and weeks. If she lasted that long.

Tuck told himself it was more of a chance than she'd given Henry of Castellford, or old Elias, but the kindly friar's heart was heavy, and he wished the Disciples of God had never come to Yorkshire. That none of this had happened.

"D'you think they'll be alright now? The Disciples I mean?" Scarlet asked.

"Without their Holy Mother, and Black Lords to battle and so on," Tuck replied, "I expect they'll drift apart, and the sect will eventually dwindle away to nothing." He shrugged. "But at least it will be of their own free will."

"Come on," grunted John, standing up and drawing his cloak around him. "It's time we went home ourselves. We'll catch up with Colwin and Margaret, and hope the snow stays off so we can get back home before the sun goes down."

There were no arguments from either Tuck or Scarlet and, as they mounted up and rode out the eastern gate towards Wakefield, the three men thanked God for their good fortune in surviving this adventure with the Disciples of God.

The mood was melancholy for, although they had all been part of brutal fights, and killed many enemies over the years, none of this business with the Lady Alice and her acolytes had been pleasant. Still, life would go on as it always did, and Brother Colwin, Sister Margaret and the rest of the group living in St Joseph's would, God willing, find a way to survive and prosper in peace and happiness.

"Well," Little John said as the sun came out from behind iron-grey clouds for a few moments, bathing the travellers in light and warmth and revealing Colwin and Margaret on the road not far ahead. "That's two strange mysteries we've managed to straighten out in the past couple of years, Tuck— we're getting pretty good at it! And, I must admit, you were a fine help this time as well, Scarlet."

Will smiled. "Aye, I suppose we did some good."

"I'd say so," the bailiff said. "Even if Lady Alice de Staynton might not agree."

"At least Amber will be happy," Tuck said.

"What do you mean?" John asked, confused at the mention of his wife.

"She was worried the Disciples would be left to fend for themselves, remember? But I think Colwin and Margaret will take good care of them for as long as it's needed. At least that's one bright spot in what's been a dark year for Yorkshire."

They all nodded in agreement and rode on, until another thought suddenly struck the friar. "Wait a minute, though, John," he said with some excitement. "In all the fuss, you've forgotten about someone."

The bailiff glanced across at him, brow furrowed. "I don't like the sound of that. Who are you talking about?"

"The fellow who pretended to be a barber-surgeon. The man from Altofts that you've had incarcerated in Altofts all this time."

John shrugged. "Clibert. What about him."

"He's not been found guilty of any crime, so he should be set free."

"Bugger him," Scarlet said forcefully. "Let him rot. He played his part in all of this and might even have been with the group that attacked Elias."

Tuck looked at John who smiled. "He's got a point. I expect the people of Altofts will let the bastard go eventually. Once the money for his keep runs out."

"Not if someone sends a few coins to pay for another month or two's meals," Scarlet said with a wicked grin and all three laughed, feeling their spirits lift, even if just a little, at the thought of Clibert's well-earned predicament.

They soon caught up with Colwin's mount, greeting him and Sister Margaret gladly and, as they all continued towards home, the snow started falling once more and Tuck wondered if there would be more mysteries to solve in the coming months and years.

Somehow, he knew there would be.

THE END

AUTHOR'S NOTE

As always, I hope you enjoyed reading this book which was supposed to run to about 20-30,000 words, like *Knight of the Cross, Friar Tuck & the Christmas Devil* and *Faces of Darkness* all did. This one is rather longer, perhaps because the addition of Will Scarlet to the team led to more things happening. Certainly, I didn't feel like the higher word count made the story any less engaging or fast-paced than my previous Forest Lord novellas, but that will be up to you, the reader, to decide!

Sworn to God came about, like *Faces of Darkness* before it, from my listening to true crime podcasts. This time it was the strange case of Terri Hoffmann and her Cult of Conscious Development that I heard about. This group was active in the USA during the 1970's and 80's and a large number of the cult's members disappeared without trace or killed themselves under strange circumstances – usually leaving all their worldly goods behind to the cult's leader. Hoffmann herself was never found guilty of playing any criminal part in those events, but it all seemed rather suspicious to most investigators – why would a healthy person commit suicide, leaving a note saying they believed they had a terminal illness and wanted to bequeath all their wealth to Hoffmann, for example? And those "Black Lords"? Yep, the Cult of Conscious Development really did claim to fight them, with some acolytes even using cocktail sticks as swords! What a strange sight those meetings must have been... Terri Hoffmann was clearly a charismatic individual who could make her followers believe the most outlandish, bizarre things.

It was a fascinating and terribly sad tale to learn about and I thought it would make an interesting case for Tuck and friends to investigate.

It's all too easy for outsiders to look at cults and think "what a bunch of bloody weirdos", and mock the mental weakness that draws people to the charismatic individuals who prey upon them, but I wanted to try and humanize those sad souls a bit. If someone's struggling with life—had a bereavement, drug or alcohol issues, low self-esteem or whatever—it's understandable that they can be drawn into what seems, at first, like a loving, supportive group. Life can be hard after all. But, when it becomes clear that the person they've become attached to isn't quite the kindly leader they thought, they're so deeply into their new life that it's impossible to escape.

In reality, of course, cults such as Heaven's Gate and the Peoples Temple, caused the deaths of hundreds of people but their leaders never had to face Earthly justice for their actions. I did not want that to be the case in *Sworn to God* – I like my books to have a proper ending, whether it's a "happy" one or not, and the "baddies" should have to deal with the consequences of their crimes. So, although in 1329 religious heresy was nowhere near the problem it would become in the later medieval period with the dreaded Inquisition, there *had* been cases in Europe of so-called heretics being beaten, burned at the stake, or exiled for their teachings. Indeed, one group of German heretics, about thirty of them, were excommunicated and branded on the forehead sometime around 1165 in Hereford. They were then driven out into the wilderness where they were to receive no aid from anyone in the land, on pain of their own house being burned down should their charity be discovered! So, Lady Alice de Staynton could certainly face a similar punishment for her heretical actions (real or invented), thanks to our intrepid heroes.

My next book will, I think, be the fourth in my Warrior Druid of Britain series. I hope you'll look out for it and, no doubt later in 2021, further adventures for Tuck, John and Will! **Stay safe everyone, and thank you so much for reading.**

Steven A. McKay,
Old Kilpatrick,
October 8th, 2020

Printed in Great Britain
by Amazon